It runs like clockwork.
Traditional

MOVES SO FAR
from Vol 1 *Law of the Wolf Tower*

1) Claidi steals a book to write about her unpleasant days in the luxurious House and Garden. Life here is lived by inflexible rules, for breaking one of which her parents were cast into the Waste. At sixteen, Claidi is herself the maid-servant of Jade Leaf, whose hobbies seem to be bad poetry and beating her maids.

2) A hot-air balloon is shot down by the House Guards. Out of it they drag handsome Prince Nemian.

3) The important Old Lady, Jizania Tiger, informs Claidi that Claidi is herself a princess. Her mother, (Twilight Star) was exiled for falling in love with her steward, Claidi's father. Jizania suggests Claidi should rescue Nemian, and go with him to his powerful city. Though uncertain, Claidi takes the chance.

4) The House exaggerated about the Waste. Even so there are dust storms, poisoned water, and treacherous Sheepers who cheerfully barter Claidi as a sacrifice. Claidi also begins to see Nemian is unfair, useless, and keen on any girl but herself.

5) Rescued by the Hulta, a wild yet honourable travelling people, Claidi learns to ride, ignores Nemian, and tries not to become fascinated by the Hulta's young Leader, Argul. (But Argul was left a chemical gadget by his dead

scientist mother, which has shown him Claidi is the woman for him.)

6) After negotiating a vegetable forest complete with monster, they reach the city of Peshamba among meadows of flowers. Here are technical surprises, including life-size mechanical dolls handy with swords.

7) Just before Claidi and Argul can admit what they feel for each other, Nemian suddenly begs Claidi not to desert him. Seeing his panic is real, she miserably agrees to go on with him to his city.

8) Nemian and Claidi reach the bleak stone City, and his home, the Wolf Tower – where she discovers he is happily married. It is the Tower which wants her, to replace Nemian's cruel grandmother, the Old Lady, Ironel, as giver of the Wolf Tower Law.

9) The Law is appalling. Read by means of giant dice and ancient, unfathomable books, it forces selected citizens to carry out mindless and often horrifying tasks. Failure to obey is mercilessly punished. (Now Claidi learns why Nemian had been afraid to lose her. It was the *Law* which said he must bring her back.) Claidi apparently gives in, and becomes Law-giver – the Wolf's Paw.

10) Argul however has followed her, intent on rescue. Rather than obey the rules Claidi destroys the Law from within, before she and he escape the city for the free world beyond.

CONTENTS

THIS BOOK, AGAIN . . .

Are you still there?

No, of course you're not. How could you be? You were never there in the first place. I made you up, selfishly, to help me feel less alone. Someone to confide in, the most trustworthy friend I ever had.

Of course, then, too, there was a chance someone might read it, this book. But surely, no one ever will, *here*. Or if they do, what I write will be some sort of weird curiosity, something to sneer at, amazedly. So it would be best to destroy this book, wouldn't it, instead of picking it up to write in again . . . after I thought I'd *never* write in it again –

Only I remember, when I left the Tower in the City, I took these extra ink pencils and pens. As if I knew I'd go on writing. But that was a reflex.

Naturally, once Argul and I (and Mehmed and Ro) got back with the Hulta, and we'd moved far enough away from the City, and there was some time – then I did write up the last bit. I remember it was a sunny afternoon on a hill, and Argul and some others had gone hunting, so I stayed where I was, and finished the story.

I explained about how I destroyed the name-cards and the volumes of numbers, and all that evil stupid junk that made up the Law in the Wolf Tower. Burnt them. And burnt my message in the wall: NO MORE LAW. And about how Argul got me away, and then we saw the City let off all those fantastic fireworks, celebrating its freedom. And I thought after that there'd be nothing much to write, because though I could cover page after page saying *Argul, Argul, Argul*, how wonderful he is, how happy *I* am – I could *live* that, didn't need to write it.

I did think I might put down an account of our wedding day, so I could look at it years later, my dress, Argul's clothes, our vows, what we ate, what everyone said, and the games and dances – that kind of thing. A keepsake.

Well, I can't even do that, can I. The marriage never happened. And Argul –

I suppose, if you did exist, and were still patiently reading, you'd prefer me to tell you all this in the right order.

But . . . maybe I won't do it just yet . . .

THE UN-WEDDING DAY

That morning the weather was beautiful. Teil said it would be, the night before, because of the sunset.

'*Red sky at set,*
Sheepers not wet.'

'Excuse me?'

'Oh Claidi. Don't you know that old rhyme?'

'I only know about the Sheepers being very dodgy. And anyway, their language is all baa-baa-baa!'

'Well, yes. But it's an ancient *translated* saying of theirs. A red sunset means it won't rain tomorrow. Which is perfect for your wedding day.'

Then Dagger strode into the tent. She'd just turned eight years old two days before, and looked fiercely motherly.

'Claidi – I want you to have this.'

'Oh – but Dagger – it's your dagger.'

'Yes. You can peel oranges with it really well, too.'

I put it in pride of place with the other things – I wish I'd kept it by me. I don't expect it would have made much difference.

People had been bringing me gifts for the past six days. It's the Hulta custom, so the bride can build up her store of useful things for her wagon. But really Argul's wagon had tons of everything, pots, plates, knives, clothes (some of which had been his late mother's, when she was young, and fitted me.) There were even books, I mean printed ones.

Still, the gifts touched me. I felt shy. I was an outsider, but no one ever made me feel that. Once Argul wanted me, and they'd seen a bit of who I was, they made me part of the Hulta family.

Wonderful to be *liked*. As opposed to having some special horrible power over people, as in the City, when I'd been Wolf's Paw, that short, foul while.

Anyway, Argul arrived then, and we went to supper at the camp's central fire.

I remember – won't ever forget – the firelight glowing on faces, the last scarlet at the sky's edge, jokes, stars, eyes gleaming in bushes and Ro wanting to throw a stone because they were 'leopards', only they weren't, they were fireflies –

And alone with Argul, and how he said, 'Are you happy? You look happy, Claidi. Cleverly disguising your misery, no doubt.'

'Yes, I've been just crying my eyes out at the thought of marrying you.'

'Mmn. Me too.'

'Shall we call it off?'

'Can't disappoint the rest of them,' he gloomily said.

We held our faces in grim expressions. I burst out laughing first.

'I never thought I'd keep you,' he said. 'You're such a maddening, mad little bird.'

'Mad, I'll accept. Maddening. I'm not so little.'

'I could put you in a nutshell and carry you about in one hand,' he said, 'oh Claidi-baa-baa!'

I remember my wedding dress. Well, I suppose I can say about that. After all, like Argul's ring, it's even here with me. I came away in it.

It's white, with embroidered patterns of green leaves. White for luck and green for spring, the Hulta bride's wedding colours. And Argul was to wear sun-yellow, for summer, the groom's colours. (Spring and summer were seasons. We don't really have them now.)

With his tea-colour skin and black hair, he would have looked incredibly splendid.

Only I never saw that.

No.

Anyway, the night was cool and still, and in the morning the sun came up and the sky was golden clear, and it was warm, as Teil had promised.

We'd been travelling about fifty, sixty days, since leaving Nemian's City.

First there'd been the flat grey plain by the River, and the thin mountains in the distance. Then we'd crossed the River, which was probably only *r*iver by then, by an old bridge I hadn't noticed when Nemian and I came down that way – or else it was higher up, beyond the marsh. (I didn't notice quite a bit of the journey.) Next we turned more south, and then our wagons were in another of those desert areas, which went on and on (only this time, with Argul, I didn't care.)

The weather gradually got nicer, though. Lots of sunny days. Then there were grasslands, not as pretty or lush as at Peshamba, but still lovely. There were stretches of woods and orchards in blossom, and streamlets gloogling merrily by, and deer feeding and other dapply things with long necks, whose names I can't recall. We held races. (Siree, my black mare, went so fast I actually won *twice*.)

There were villages too, made of painted wood, with grass-thatched roofs. Smiling people came out waving, and we bartered with them. And once there was a big stone circle on a hill, where no one could go in, only stand outside and look, because a wind god lived there, they said.

Then the land just sort of flowed, with the breezy grass running round islands of hills and trees, in sunlight. Argul said we were now only twenty miles from the sea, and I'd never seen a sea. We'd go there, said Argul. But first we'd have our wedding, and use the grassy plain as our dancing-floor, because the Hulta marriage dances stir up flowers, and make trees grow – or so the Hulta boastfully say.

Oh.

You may as well know, a tear nearly thumped on the page. Damn.

(I never used to swear. I wouldn't, because the nasty royalty in the House, where I was a slave-maid, were always swearing, and I didn't want to be like them.)

Anyway if I'm going to cry and swear I'll stop writing. So that's that.

(I think I do have to write this down. I don't know why.

Like a spell or something. But I'm not so daft that I think it will *help* in any way.)

On the wedding morning it's thought bad luck if a Hulta groom and bride see each other. But – well, we did. But we only laughed and separated quickly for custom's sake. Didn't even really kiss each other good-bye – had no reason to, of course. (Every reason to, if we'd known.)

I went first to groom Siree. Ashti and I plaited Siree's mane and tail with green and silver ribbons. I'd ride her to my wedding. A Hulta bride always rides.

After that *I* had to be groomed.

There was this terrific private pool Dagger had found in the woods, and Teil and Toy and Dagger and Ashti and I went there to bathe and wash our hair. We took our wedding clothes, and the jewels and make-up and everything, plus some hot bread and fruit juice and sweets. I'd brought this book, too, and an ink pencil, to jot stuff down – although I didn't really think I'd have time.

The trees grew in close around the pool, but above there was a scoop of cloudless sky. Flower-bells in the water.

Brides are supposed to be nervous. I wasn't, just happy. But our game was that I was really upset and scared, and somehow we got into a story, splashing around in the pool, about how Argul was a dreadful bully about sixty years old, who'd unhitch the horses and make me pull the wagon, with his other *six* wives.

In the middle of this, I looked up, and saw it go over. Then the other two.

I just stood there in the water, and I went – not cold, kind of *stony*.

'She's just properly realized it's that hideous hundred-year-old Argul she's got to marry!' screamed Ashti.

They all yowled and splashed me.

'No – I saw –'

'She's so frightened, now she's *seeing* things!'

Dagger said, 'Shut up – what was it, Claidi?'

But they'd gone.

'I must have – imagined – I don't know.'

Teil looked stern. 'You do. What?'

'Balloons.'

They went blank. Then realization dawned.

'You mean like from the grey City –'

'Well – not really. I mean I only ever saw one from there, and these weren't the same.'

That was true. Nemian's balloon had been silvery, round. These were more sort of mushroom shaped, a dull coppery colour.

Had I imagined it? Had they been some odd, big, new kind of insect that looked larger but farther up?

In any case, many places had fleets of hot air balloons, Nemian had always been going on about that. Peshamba had had them . . . or hadn't they?

Though the sky was still cloud-clear, a sort of shadow had fallen. We got out, not really dry, shoved on our best clothes. Even my wedding dress got put on fast, without much care. (Without thinking I thrust this book in my pocket.) Shaking out our wet hair, we went up through the trees, leaving most of our picnic, and everything else.

The main camp wasn't much more than a quarter of a mile away. Not that far. (Only, down a slope, through all the trees.) It hadn't seemed to matter earlier.

Argul knew all about what had happened in the Wolf Tower and the City, and what I'd done. Mehmed and Ro had some idea, but weren't really that bothered. I'd never discussed it with anyone else, nor had they pestered to know. They seemed to accept it was something I'd prefer to forget.

Only now Teil said, quietly, 'Claidi, is it possible they might have sent someone after you?'

'Me?' But it was no good being modest. I'd wrecked the Wolf Tower Law. The fireworks had seemed to prove most of the City was glad about that. But I'd had some doubts. The Old Lady, for one, Ironel, what about her? I'd never been sure, there. 'It's – possible.'

We began to walk quickly, not running, in the direction we'd come, back towards the camp.

And then, the strangest sound, behind us.

I thought afterwards it was only startled birds, lots of them, flying up and away. Then, it sounded as if the wood had sprouted wings and was trying to escape. The light and shade were all disturbed, with fluttering and flickering, and then there was a thud behind us.

Something had come down – landed.

None of us said anything or yelled. We all just broke into a run.

Instantly every single tree-root and bush and creeper in the wood seemed to come jumping up to trip and sprawl us.

But over the chorus of panting and crashes and yelps, and Dagger's always impressive bagful of rude words – another *thud*. This one was quite close.

The light had altered. Something was blotting it up . . . A brownish reddishness, and on the ground a huge shadow, cruising – and I looked up, having tripped again, and a balloon hung there, right over the trees.

It looked *enormous*. Like a dirty bloated fallen sun. No, like a copper thunder-cloud –

And then – I don't know really what happened. I've tried

to piece it together, can't, as if somehow I've *forgotten* those completely crucial moments.

But it was as if the wood changed again. This time all the trees became *men*.

They were in uniform, white, or black, with plates of metal, and *guns*, and I ridiculously thought *The House Guards*!

They must have grabbed hold of me. I was in a sort of metal web, and I couldn't see where Teil and Dagger and the others were. As I kicked and tried to bite I hoped they'd got away. And I thought, They'll get help – and then, *Anyway, someone will have seen* – but the camp had been so busy – getting ready for the wedding. And these woods were uphill. And the trees –

Then one of the armoured men said to me, 'Stop struggling, or you'll wish you had.'

They weren't House Guards. But I knew that tone, those words. He meant what he said. (It was useless anyway.) I became quite still.

Another one said, 'Is this the one?'

'It's *her*,' said the first one, who must be the one who had hold of me in the web. 'I saw her almost every day in the City.'

'He'd never forget,' said the other, 'would you, Chospa? Not after she made such a blazing great fool of you.'

'Chospa' growled and shook me angrily, and the chain-web rattled. Who was he? Just one of several enemies from my past –

Then there were shouts of 'Haul away!'

And to my disbelieving horror *I* was being hauled upwards, up through the slapping branches of the trees, so I had to protect my eyes – up into the air. Up to the disgusting balloon.

I kept thinking, someone will come in a moment. Argul

and the Hulta had rescued me before – once, twice – Argul will rush in gorgeously bellowing, and Mehmed and Ro and Blurn and everyone.

I kept thinking this even after I was pulled over into the basket under the balloon. Kept thinking it even as the balloon lifted, with a terrifying hiss of hot gas over my head. As the ground fell away. As the trees became like a clump of watercress, as I saw the Hulta camp – like a child's colourful tiny toy, spread out, peaceful, far away – too far even to see if they'd noticed.

Then suddenly, as I lay there on the balloon-basket's floor, I knew it was now too late. And then it was as if some mistake had been made and it was my fault, my mistake. Only what had I done wrong?

BALLOON RIDE

'Some girls would give their front teeth, to ride in a balloon like this,' said one of my captors haughtily, about an hour later.

So I was ungrateful, presumably?

Chospa, who was in the white uniform, glared at me under his steel helmet crested with a stiff white plume.

'Chospa's still very angry with you,' said the one in black.

I thought *I* was quite angry with *Chospa*. Or would be if I weren't so frightened, so *numbed* by what had happened.

'Look, she doesn't remember you, even, Chospa.'

'No. She never looked at me once, until that last time.'

'Tell us again, Chospa. It's always good for a laugh.'

Chospa swore.

He said, 'She was going to be *Wolf's Paw*. I *respected* her.'

'You trusted her,' said the one in black.

'We all did. Who didn't? She was absolutely correct in everything. Couldn't fault her.'

The one who'd remarked I might want to give my front teeth for this exciting ride, (I found out later his name was Hrald) said, 'But listen, boys, she'd destroyed everything, even the holy books, and then she prances down with our Chospa here, to the street. Says she wants a walk. Then she says,' (here Hrald mimicked a female – my – voice, high and stupid and squeaky, how he thinks females sound, I suppose) ' "Dooo let me see that delicious darling rifle, dearest Chospa. Ee've always admeered it sooo." And what does the dupp do, but give it to her –'

'I didn't know she'd destroyed the Law – or that she had savage barbarians waiting by the Tower door,' snarled Chospa.

I knew him now, of course.

He'd been my guard/bodyguard in the City. Meant to protect me and/or keep me prisoner.

It's true, I'd never really glanced at him. Most of the people there looked like mechanical dolls, clockwork, without minds or hearts.

I'd just been glad that night it was all being so simple, getting away.

Argul had taken the rifle from me and shut Chospa in the Tower, and I hadn't really thought about it again. Not even when I wrote down what happened.

Chospa now said, 'I couldn't open the Tower door. You can't from inside, unless it recognizes your rank – like it did hers. I had to sit there. Later I was called in to the Old Lady. I was in there, explaining, two hours.'

No one laughed at this.

Two hours with Ironel Novendot. Ironel either furiously

angry or else making believe she was. Her black eyes, snapping real-pearl teeth and poison tongue, her dry white claws. I didn't envy him. His face now, just remembering, was pale and sick-looking. (The way mine felt.)

'Lost his house in the City,' said Hrald. The one in black – his name is Yazkool, (I haven't forgotten their names, once heard. Never will, I expect) said, 'Just about kept his place in the City Guards. Allowed to come with us on our joyous quest, weren't you, Chospa, to identify Miss, here. Ironel's orders.'

(I hadn't realized he *couldn't* open the door. Thought they'd just sat there and not come after us because they were insane.) (The Tower door could *recognize* me? That was new. But so what –)

Drearily I huddled on the floor of the balloon-basket. Were they going to throw me out when we got high enough? We were high up now. No, they were going to take me back to the City, to the Tower. To *her*. And then – well.

Would Argul realize? Of course. He'd come after me, like before. Rescue me, somehow.

A spark of hope lit up bright inside me. I was careful not to let the three Guards see.

But I did sit up a bit. The web-chain had fallen off. I tried to glimpse over the basket's high rim. Couldn't see much.

Rolls of landscape, soft with distance, but down – and down – below. And the vast moving sky, with clouds like cauliflower blowing up over there, where the plain looked oddly flat and *shiny* –

It was choppy, riding in the balloon. I hadn't noticed that either, except as part of the general awfulness.

Above roared the fire-gas thing that powered the balloon. There was one more man in the basket, shifting some contraption about, (like a boat-driver) to guide the balloon, probably. I didn't understand it.

Even though I'd brightened a bit, I was hardly light-hearted or very observant. But I now noted one of the other mushroom balloons, which looked miles away. We must be going quite fast?

I felt rather queasy, but it wasn't air-sickness, more shock.

'I must say,' Hrald must-said, 'I was surprised you took all that, Chospa. I mean, the way the old bag ranted on at you.'

Even *I* was astonished. Chospa gaped. *Old bag* – Ironel!!!

'She's the Keeper of the Law,' gaped Chospa.

'Yeah, well. But she went too far. Disgraced you. What happened was her fault, too.'

'Definitely not fair,' agreed the other one, Yazkool.

Chospa shrugged, turned away. He now looked blank and mechanical again.

I saw Hrald and Yazkool exchange a glance. Hrald shook his head, seeming to say, *Don't let's upset him any more.*

The balloon-driver – ballooneer I think they call them – had looked round too. He was a short bearded man, and he gave an ugly grin. That was all.

I didn't think much about this, or anything. I was glad as I stopped feeling sick. Also concentrated on seeming resigned and meek, in case there'd be any unlikely chance later to get away.

Sometimes it felt hot in the balloon, and then chilly. We were in a chilly phase when Chospa suddenly barked out 'Tell that fool to watch what he's doing!'

'Oh, he's all right.'

'Are you blind? We're going over too far east –' and Chospa shouted at the ballooneer, 'Pull her round, you moron. The City's *that* way!'

'Calm down, Chos,' said Hrald, in a matey voice. 'Trust me, it's fine.'

'What is this?' shouted Chospa.

'Oh, we're just,' said Hrald, idling across the bumpy balloon-basket, 'going to do something, er, first –' and then he reached Chospa and punched him *whack* on the jaw. Chospa tumbled over and the basket plunged and the ballooneer cursed us all.

As we bucketed about the sky, the land dipping, clouds dipping, sun turning over, I saw we were also much lower, and that shining flat plain was gleaming everywhere to one side. It must be the sea?

Chospa rolled against me and I stared in alarm at his poor unconscious face, with the bruise already coming up like a ripe plum.

Yazkool laughed, seeing me worrying.

Hrald only said, 'Bring us down over there, that stand of pines.'

'They always want miracles,' muttered the ballooneer.

And then the air-gas-fire was making ghastly dragon-belches and we seemed to be dropping like a stone.

All around the sky was empty of anything – but sky. The other two balloons were completely out of sight.

The ground came rushing up and I thought we'd all just be killed, and was too frightened even to be sick after all, and then we landed with a bump that rattled everything, including my bones and poor old Chospa.

Well, we were fairly near the pines . . .

Next thing I knew, they were dragging me out of the basket. Yazkool unfortunately was securely tying my wrists together.

'There's the sea,' pointed out Hrald, still apparently

14

determined for me not to miss any of the travel or sight-seeing opportunities.

Beyond the hill slope we'd crash-landed on, and between the black poles of the ragged pines, a silver mass gushed and crawled. Chunks of it constantly hit together and burst in white fringes.

Argul would have shown me that. Helped me make sense of it.

It was now cold, or I felt cold. The clouds were swarming in the sky, bigger and darker and bigger.

The mushroom-pod of the balloon seemed to be deflating. No one did anything about Chospa, just let him lie there on his back.

'Then where are they?' demanded the ballooneer.

'Don't bother your pretty little head about it,' said Hrald. 'We've made good time.'

The ballooneer scowled but said nothing else. Yazkool produced a pair of nail-scissors and began neatly to trim his nails.

The wind blew, hard and spiky from the sea. I wanted to get out of the wind, so sat down, with hand-tied awkwardness, against one of the pines.

I didn't realize even then that harsh, silver-salt wind was going to be my constant companion for quite some time to come.

About half an hour later, some wild men came trudging up the hill.

They'd called the Hulta 'barbarians', as I'd have expected City people would. These really *did* look barbaric. Their clothes were all colours, all patched, mis-matched, too bright or faded, and all filthy. They had rings through their ears,

15

their noses, their eyebrows, lips, *teeth*, and beads plaited in hair, moustaches and beards. Several had one shoe or boot different to the other. There were a lot of knives, clubs and nasty-looking catapult things.

They spoke another language, too, which only Hrald seemed to have any idea of. One of them, who was dark but with very yellow hair, spoke a bit of the language the City speaks, that language I suppose is also mine.

No one mentioned me.

I had the strangest feeling that I had nothing to do with any of this. I tried to merge into the tree, but of course that was silly. Yazkool presently came and pulled me up, and I was marched down with the others towards the silver waves.

They're going to drown me, I decided. *It's some new quaint ritual.*

I'm sacrifice-material, obviously. I mean, the Sheepers saw that at once, and gave me to the Feather Tribe, who meant to sling me off a cliff. As for Jizania and Nemian, I was the best sacrifice of all to them. My life was *barter* for their royal lives, in the House and the City.

But we skirted the sea – which was very *wet*, very icy, with colours like tea and lime-juice in it now, seen so near. We went along a strip of sand and over slippery pebbles and black stones. Around a curve of headland, I saw a ship on the water. Ah, we were going to the ship.

I didn't cry. It was as if I'd known somehow this would happen.

It had to be too simple just to kidnap me and carry me off to be killed in the City, where just possibly I might escape or Argul rescue me.

No, no, I had to be *re*-kidnapped *again*, and put on this rotten ship with its mucky old stained sail, taken off somewhere with this ship's crew who all looked completely dangerously *mad*.

We rowed out in a leaky boat.

They pushed me up a ladder – not easy to climb, hands tied, shaking, the sea going *glump-whump*, everything rocking.

('Enormous seas, Claidi,' said Argul, in my mind. 'Miles of water and sky.')

Something, some bird, flew over, shrieking. A gull. I didn't know it was. I didn't ask, or care. They bundled me into a dark cabin and slammed the door, and there I was.

YET MORE TRAVEL OPPORTUNITIES

When I think about it now, I think I should just have jumped into the sea. That's what a proper heroine in one of the House books would have done. (Although naturally a handy passing boat or giant fish would then have rescued her immediately.) I'm not a heroine, anyway. I'm just Claidi.

Anyway I didn't, did I.

How long did it last, that thing they called a *voyage*? Months, years.

Oh, about twenty-five or six days, maybe. I kept count the way the (in-a-book) captive is meant to, by scratching on the cabin wall by the wooden chest. I did it promptly every morning, without fail. And then, obviously, being me, being Claidi, I *forgot* the number the moment we got off the ship.

But, about twenty-five, thirty days. Perhaps.

Oddly, I sometimes thought about Chospa. It seemed so unfair, because, through no fault of his own, he'd be in trouble all over again. I could cheerfully have punched him

17

on the nose myself, but at least he'd been honourably doing what he thought he should.

Instead of Chospa, there were Yazkool and Hrald. (The ballooneer hadn't joined the ship. I don't know what his plans were but I hope so much they went wrong.)

I hated them, Y and H. Was *allergic* to them. Not just because they'd made my escape-chances totally hopeless, either. They were so smug and − *royal* − always cleaning their nails, their teeth, brushing their hair, complaining about the way they had to 'make do' on the ship. And at the same time so *smilingly-mysterious* about what they were up to. That is, what they meant to do with me. Of course, I *had* asked.

The moment they opened the cabin and said I could come out now, since there was nowhere to go (obviously having *never* read any of those jump-overboard books *I* had) I asked them.

'Where are you taking me, and why?'

'Why not let it be a wonderful surprise?' suggested leering Yazkool.

'Tell me *now*!' I cried. I meant to sound like the Wolf's Paw, or apprentice Wolf's Paw, I'd been. I didn't manage it. The ship was also pitching about, and although I found I was (thank heavens) a good sailor (that is I didn't want to throw up) I could hardly keep on my feet − even now they'd untied my hands.

Hrald looked bored. 'I'm off below,' he said.

Yazkool beamingly said, 'Lady Claidissa, why not think of this as being an adventure for you?'

Hrald, who hadn't yet gone, added, 'And much nicer than being imprisoned for life in the City cellars, wouldn't you say?'

'How did you know where I was? How did you find

me?' I gabbled. They were already staggering, sea-legs almost as hopeless as mine, down the deck.

One of the wild sailor-people undid a hatch, and they stepped-fell through and were gone.

I made the mistake of looking round then. I didn't throw up, but I nearly screamed.

Everything was galloping and tilting this way, that way. The vast mast, with its dirty sail, seemed to keep going to crash right over on us all. Waves a hundred feet high (they can't have been, but looked it) kept exploding up in the sky and hurling spray into the ship and all over us.

No one seemed upset. Cheery sailors strode bow-leggedly up and down, or scrambled across rope-arrangements on the mast, calling merry, other-language insults, and singing.

Water sloshed down the deck, ran into the cabin, then, as we nose-dived the other way, ran out again.

In fact, it wasn't quite as bad as it looked that first time. But it took me hours to get used to it, and by then the wind had settled down a little (temporarily), and the sea was flatter. This too then happened to me. My brief anger went out. I felt flat and utterly lost.

Obviously, the 'voyage' was disgusting. It would have been, even if I'd wanted to do it.

I've read or heard these stories of glorious days on board ships. Blue waters, amazingly-shaped clouds, dolphins (?) and other fish – or sea-animal-things, leaping, the comradeship of sailors. This wasn't my experience.

The sailors fought a lot.

I think it was boredom. They never seemed to do anything useful, but they were always either rushing acrobatically about, or sitting playing dice or card games, or even peculiar guessing games (I'd picked up some of their language by then.)

Yazkool told me (he and Hrald kept coming and talking patronizingly to me, as if I should be flattered by their attention) that the sailors have nine hundred and seven words for *Sea*. Perhaps it was a lie. They certainly had about a thousand filthy words for Go Away, or Idiot! (Dagger would have loved it, memorizing them for future use.) (I mustn't think too much about Dagger. Or Siree. Or anyone. Not now. I refuse – I REFUSE – to think I won't see them again. But . . . it won't be for a long while.)

Anyway, the sailors were rowdy. H and Y strolled about, discussing how shirts were cut and trimmed in the City that year, or how this water was too salty to shave properly. Some days the sea was blue – but never for long. Storms came regularly. Hrald, (another lecture) told me it was the Stormy Season.

Once or twice, when they cornered me, I confronted them.

'Did you both *enjoy* life in the Wolf Tower City?' I demanded.

'What other life is there?' drawled Yazkool.

'At any moment,' I yapped, 'the Tower Law could have picked you out for some terrible fate.'

'Oh, it did once. I had to marry some girl.'

What could I say to that? *I'd* seen the Law force a child to wear, day and night, the costume of a snail, with the *shell*. Or send a man swimming up and down the River, allowed only to rest briefly, when 'exhausted', *for ever*.

'It's probably nicer there now,' I acidly remarked, 'since I stopped the Law.'

'It's much the same,' said Yazkool. What an okk.

Hrald said, 'Anyhow, the Law may be re-invented.'

That shut me up. I hadn't thought of that.

Surely it would be *impossible*? All those names to gather again – besides there had only been single copies of the Books of Law – and I'd destroyed them. Or had Ironel lied to me? Were there other copies? I nearly burst into tears, this idea was so depressing. I wouldn't let *them* see, of course. I looked out to sea, as if indifferent, and said, 'Well, if your City is stupid enough to do that, it serves you all right.'

Which was, and is, true. I'd given them a chance, more than they'd had since the Law began. A chance is just about all you ever get.

The cabin (I'd seen a cabin before, on the river ship which first carried me to the City) was quite large. I had it to myself. From that I decided, wherever they were taking me, they were supposed to take care of me. Not damage me or insult me beyond a certain point. (As if being abducted wasn't the worst thing they could have done, short of killing me.)

There was a (lumpy) bed and the wooden chest, with things in it that had fairly obviously been put there for my 'comfort'.

In the wall (the ship's side) was a round window, glass criss-crossed with iron, through which I could admire the endless jumping dolphin-less sea.

I didn't stay in the cabin very much.

When I did, I could be private. (H and Y brought me meals, I didn't have much to do with the sailors, or wasn't allowed to.) But when alone, I sometimes started to cry. Well.

So I tended to go out on deck, where people could see me, and I had to *not* cry.

I did glance at this book a couple of times. Wondered if I ought to write in it, couldn't bring myself to.

Argul knew about this book. (Nemian had called it my 'Diary'. He would. It wasn't. Isn't. I don't know what it is. My long letter to you, perhaps, if you ever read it.)

Argul just accepted I'd written things down in a book. He didn't ask about it or want to read it. Yet he wasn't dismissive either. But that was . . . well, Argul.

Argul.

I took it with me to the wood pool because I was going to write down a few things about my wedding day, some as they happened.

And when we left the pool, I stuffed it in the pocket of my Wedding Dress, which by three days into the voyage was spoilt, dirty, sea-stained and torn.

The horrible idea I keep getting is that I brought this book with me to the pool, and then put it in my pocket – not out of old habit, but because I somehow knew *this* would happen.

Y and H were having lunch on deck, in an odd hour of sunshine.

Blue sky and sea. Gentle lilts from the ship. Even the sailors were mostly below at a meal and quiet.

I went and sat with my captors. They instantly made room for me. Y even passed me a glass of wine. They'd actually *expected* me some time to come over to them – the extra glass, their unsurprise. I mean, they'd ruined my life, but they were so *wonderful*, how could I go on ignoring them?

'You see, it's a nice day today, Claidissa.'

(They always call me that, my full name, which I'd only learned months before, and not got used to – or was ever sure I liked.)

'Is it?'

22

'She's never satisfied,' said Yazkool, who, as I approached, had been going on and on (again) about the salty shaving water.

'How strange, isn't it,' I said, 'that I'm not satisfied. Everything's so lovely, isn't it? I'm kidnapped and trapped on a stormy ship and going I don't know where or why or to what. Funny me. Wow.'

Then I wished I hadn't spoken. They'd think I was trying to have a conversation with them, flirting even. (They both think they're gorgeous. They aren't. Oh well, to be fair, they might have been all right, under other circumstances.)

Hrald said, however, 'No, we've been childish, haven't we, you must be miserable.' Then he grinned, naturally.

Yazkool said, 'You see, Claidissa, the City was all rejoicing and fireworks, but the people at the Top,' (it had a capital T as he said it) 'they weren't happy. You have to have rules, Claidissa. Or where would we all be, I ask you?'

The people at the Top? Who? Ironel – I thought she was at the Top. Nemian – no. Though a prince, he was just as much a slave, in a way, as I was, to the Law.

Did it matter anyway.

Only the result mattered. This.

Hrald finished picking at his food, pushed plates aside. He took out one of those City dainties, a twig-thing from a little gold box. Once he'd eaten the twig he lit one of the long black stems of packed tobacco they smoked in the City, a thing they called a *beetle*. (I *don't* know why. The first time I heard Nemian say, on the river ship, he was just going to light a *beetle* I'd gone rigid.)

'In a few more days,' said Hrald, 'we'll reach land.'

'Unless another really bad storm crops up,' optimistically added Yazkool.

'Then, we go inland,' said H.

'More exciting travel. How blissful.'

'Yes, an interesting trip,' said H.

It occurs to me, perhaps H and Y are less sarcastic and cruel than plain thick.

'Why?' I said again.

'You'll soon find out. Don't be so concerned. You see the trouble we've gone to. You're valuable, therefore valued. No one's even stolen that gaudy diamond ring of yours.'

'Then what do you get out of this?' I inquired. 'I mean, *you've* annoyed the Wolf Tower now, haven't you? They had me captured, and you re-captured me. What about these Top People?'

'Mmm,' said H. He blew a smoke-ring. Typical.

Just then Y slipped an arm about me and I turned and slapped him really hard across his still-beautifully-shaven, rotten face.

Some sailors had come up from below and now went into great gouts of glee. The dark one with yellow hair called out something, which I think meant, 'Hey, she *bites*!'

Which brought memories, and I got up and went to the cabin and shut myself in.

Ages after, when the sea was getting rough, again, and the sky and the window purplish, I thought, But *why* am I valuable?

No answer to that.

I started wondering again if Teil and Dagger, Ashti and Toy had got away from the other balloons and their riders. Then again I had that nagging unease.

How did the balloons know where to find me? Well, yes, they could have spotted the big Hulta camp from the air just by careful searching. But to come to the *pool*, where I was almost alone? Dagger had found the pool. Teil suggested we go there. Betrayal? Not Dagger. Not Teil. Not Toy or Ashti either. Ashti is Blurn's girlfriend, and Blurn was my friend – Argul's second-in-command and –

How can I be sure?

About anything.

In the finish, the 'voyage' just seemed as if it would never end. Then there was a really frightening storm. The sky went green as spinach. The sea was black.

Yazkool got seasick. It was one of my few moments of pleasure. Then I even felt a bit sorry for him. (There's something wrong with me.)

The sailors were scared. They took in the sail and tied themselves to the mast or the helm. They weren't swearing! Waves broke gigantic on the deck, and the men were baling water out in buckets, and then H came and pushed me back in the cabin and locked the door from the outside. I thought I'd probably drown.

Finally all the noise died down, and the sailors started swearing again.

When I was let out, the deck was still awash. The sea was now green, but the waves playful more than murderous. The sky was pure gold, thinking itself into after-storm sunset.

And there across all this vista, was a shadowy gilded hem on the sky's lowest edge, that I thought was a cloud. Until I made out the sailor's word (they apparently have one) for *land*.

Y was still heaving dedicatedly over the side.

H strolled up.

'*There* you are, you see,' he announced proudly, as if he'd done just what I'd begged him to.

We came ashore in our old chum, the leaky boat. Actually it almost sank just before we got to the beach.

I'd anticipated something else. In books I'd come across seaside docks and ports, with towns or villages attached. I'd thought the ship would go somewhere like that. It hadn't. Also, we left the ship at dusk, and only the dark sailor with blond hair, who H and Y called Bat-Nose (!), and one other one, rowed us.

The land had faded from the light and grown black, with the sun vanishing behind it to the left. The sky was deep red, magenta, then quickly darkening. Stars sparkled out.

Above the sandy beach, which ran back and back, more than twenty man-heights-lying-down, was a forest. A wall of trees, where strange (bird?) calls sounded and then went quiet. I didn't see much of all this, the light went so fast, or seemed to. But the forest didn't look like any forest I'd seen, not in the Garden, or at Peshamba. More than luxuriant it was – *fat*.

Bat-Nose and the other one (I think he was called, in his own language, Charming) lit a fire. We sat down round it, all except Y, who was still sick and had fallen in a heap, refusing to talk.

On the sea, the ship twinkled a lamp at us, like a fallen star.

I looked at it dubiously.

Not that I was fond of the ship. But I'd got used to it. Physically too, the beach felt a bit roll-y. And where now?

I slept apart, rolled up in two blankets, though the night wasn't cold, but I didn't want to share the fire with *them*.

During the night I woke once. Something absolutely terrifying. A shadow-*something* was prowling along the beach. It looked rather like a lion, but paler, and with a sort of

26

snake-skin-like patterning on its pelt that a young moon had risen to show me.

It went to the margin of the sea, and sniffed at the waves – or drank them or something, only they were salty . . . Then it glided back, and threaded through the sprawl of sleepers round the dying fire.

They'd been too lazy to set anyone to watch. Too smug. Too smug even to wake up and yell.

I wondered if the ghostly cat would attack them, but it didn't. To me it paid no attention at all.

In the end it trotted back up the beach and vanished in the forest. Took me ages to doze again.

Next morning they were all in a flap, because there were its pad-marks in the sand inches away.

Bat-Nose and Charming cast me unliking looks.

Y, now mostly recovered, announced this to me: the sailors thought *I* had changed into a 'white tigapard' in the night.

I pointed out that if that had been the case, I'd hardly have hung around.

It's called a Jungle. A jungle-forest, this forest.

I'd never seen anything like it, not seen a picture like it, or even a description.

The trees are about two hundred feet high, or higher. Miles high, perhaps.

And at the top, mostly, they close together, so there's a ceiling of foliage.

The light is almost wet-green, but often most like a soupy green dusk. Sometimes there is a break in the leaf-canopy, and the sky is there, but looking almost colourless, luminous yet somehow *unlit*.

Lower down, apart from boughs and leaves, (plump, juicy

leaves, or long whippy leaves, or dense fans of leaves) there are creepers and vines, many thicker than a man's arm. Some have flowers, trumpet-shaped, or petal-plates. They're pale generally, because of the lack of proper light. Higher up, you glimpse brighter ones, where thin trails of light pierce through, flashes of crimson, turquoise or tangerine.

But the flowers could be birds, too, because the jungle-forest is full of birds, some very small and some very big, and all of them all colours. There are also monkeys, and other tree-swingers. Silent as shadows or else shriekingly, jumpmakingly noisy.

On the ground grow great clumps of black-green fern, often taller than I am, or bamboos, which I'd seen at the House, but not like these – these were taller than tall Yazkool.

Perhaps most important, all the vegetation constantly knits itself together. The vines are using the bamboos to curl round and so climb from tree trunk to trunk. The trees root in each other. Other creepers come unwound high up, and loop down and get caught by ferns. Ferns grab high boughs and sprout forty feet up.

Through these attachments weave other things – ivies and grasses and funguses and blue-white orchids – all trying to climb up each other and reach the light. Any traveller has to hack his way much of the time with broad-bladed knives.

Once you're in the middle of all this, if ever you can see far through any occasional gap, the jungle weaves on and around into the distance.

It goes on for ever in all directions. Or seems to. Sometimes a huge rocky hill may go staggering up out of everything, with trees leaning out sideways from it. But although a hill, it's smothered too by jungle, and its summit won't break through the canopy, only make part of the canopy from all its particular high trees.

Once there was a shower of rain. We heard it pattering above. Not a single drop fell through.

Just after the business about the tigapard on the beach, three men appeared out of the trees.

I've thought since, how did they know to meet Y and H just there? The storm had surely blown the ship away from any course she (they're called 'she'!) might have had. And the shore where we'd landed was quite a distance from the jungle-road which we eventually reached.

None of that occurred to me then. It just seemed horribly inevitable.

Two of the newcomers were slaves, the kind I'd seen at the House, and in the City, though these were dressed in absolute rags. It was so warm and humid, even by night, maybe their master didn't think that mattered so much.

This other man, presumably the master, wore extravagant clothes, all colours (like the parrots in the trees) and with fringes, tassels, bells, buttons, holes cut out and embroidered. He jingled as he moved, but he had a hard face, like a brown nut no one could crack.

'Hallo there, Zand,' greeted Yazkool and Hrald. Then everyone started speaking mostly in yet another language.

Presently we went into the jungle. (Bat-Nose and Charming didn't go with us.)

There was an instant clearing, with two more slaves (in rags) and a round hooped openwork little carriage. It was drawn by two stripy deer with horns. There were other, bigger deer, with antlers, in reins and saddles.

Hrald said, 'Man, do we ride *those*?' looking haughty.

The antlered deer snorted and looked even haughtier.

They put me in the carriage. I didn't try to tell them I could probably have ridden as well. The deer seemed less reasonable than my lovely mare, Siree. Well, they were *deer*.

I didn't even laugh at Hrald, slipping about all over his deer, which at once bucked and cantered about, taking extra pains to cause him trouble. Like a mule, really.

One of the slaves drove my carriage. His rags were a bit nicer, and he was black, like Blurn, but without any of Blurn's quick wit or good looks. Of course, they all looked ugly and hateful to me. Maybe they weren't.

At first the other three slaves went in front, hacking a way through the undergrowth and creepers. Sometimes it got so bad my driver, and then Zand, Hrald and Yazkool, had to join in the hackery.

Should I have slipped out of the carriage then and run away into the forest?

I vaguely considered it once or twice. But the jungle just looked – was – impassable. And where could I go? I was totally lost.

I should wait until I knew more, had learned more. Did I say that to myself? I think I just sat there.

Of course, the jungle was (is) fascinating.

Sometimes I'd feel a dart of real interest – those monkeys with velvet-black faces, yet white on their hand-paws and lower arms, like long white gloves. That huge snake twined round and round a fig tree; there seemed more snake than tree. For a split glimmer of a second I'd almost be *happy*. Forgetting. Only for a split second.

Soon we reached the road.

Zand seemed proud of the road, as if he had personally designed it, and then built it himself. Which I doubt.

It wasn't much, anyway, not any more. Stone paving about

three lying-down-man-heights across . . . eighteen feet, maybe. But the jungle-forest was busily seeding all over it. Trees and shrubs grew out of it, closed over it above. And in places it had been entirely swallowed.

So then hack-hack, curse-curse, moan-whinge-whine.

Yazkool was the worst.

'I didn't *know* this would be so *primitive*!'

Or was Hrald worst? 'I could have been at home, you know, in my tower, civilized. Playing the mandolin.'

(The idea that Hrald plays the mandolin is incredibly infuriating. I can just see him, in that stone City of Law and miseries, smilingly plincking away.)

This part of the journey took, not years, but a whole century.

Perhaps only a month.

Sometimes we saw more big cat-like animals, which made an impact on the deer (so they were even more difficult) and on Yazkool, who seemed to want to kill them, not to protect us, or to eat, but just for their spectacular skins.

Then, once or twice through those choked gaps in the trees, there were ruins of buildings.

At first I thought they were only pieces of other overgrown rock-hills. But some had carved roofs and columns. And once there was a huge stone statue of a robed woman, about twenty feet high – I'm not exaggerating or guessing, Zand told us all its height, showing off again, as if *he* had carved it. But it was older than Zand. Older than even Ironel had said she was, which was one hundred and seventy. That statue was hundreds, thousands of years old.

But I wasn't in the mood for rare plants, animals, and educational ancient ruins. Or for any of this guided tour which had been forced on me.

The worst part is that it's still going on, in a way, because it's still right there now, jungle, stones, beasts, right outside this high window.

For anyway, at long last, my captors brought me *here*.

HERE

By the morning we arrived, I'd given up the notion of ever arriving anywhere. It was very silly, but I just thought we'd go rambling on and on until everyone died of boredom or anxiety or both.

Then we were bumbling along the road, which was more overgrown than ever. The deer were frisky and Hrald was grumbling. Hack-hack went the knives. Then a greenish glow came through the tunnel over the road, the last creepers gave way and last bamboo collapsed.

The world yawned wide.

After all the closed-inness, this abyss of space and sunlight was almost unbearable.

Colossal openness. Above, the shell of a white-blue sky, ringing with sun.

Everything hazed in sun, and *spray* – although at first I didn't see why. There was too *much* to see.

'Behold!' announced Zand, in his own language.

He'd invented and built this too, of course.

Out of the jungles rose and rose, soaring upwards, a cliff of yellowish stone, bulging, pocked and cracked, and clambered by huge trees that looked small as grass blades.

It did seem the widest tallest thing I'd ever looked at. Higher and mightier than any city. And much more magnificent.

There was a rushing roar, which I'd heard faintly for so long, getting ever louder, but by tiny degrees, so I'd never really heard it, or understood I had.

It was a waterfall.

The House had had them. A fountain made to tip from a height, cascading over and down. The best one was above Hyacinth Lawn. It was about two storeys high.

This waterfall, here, began way up on the towering cliff. It burst out of the rocks, which were lost in a blue fog. Then it fell, tons of liquid, straight and *solid* as a pillar, yet it smoked and steamed from bounced-back water – and the spray, which filled the ravines and valleys below as if something was on fire.

Rainbows hung across the gulf of air, bridges we couldn't cross.

Everyone had gone quiet. Even Y and H were impressed. It turned out they hadn't seen the cliff before, or the waterfall.

Hrald didn't even give me one of his guided-tour remarks.

I expect anyone else would have been thrilled, despite themselves, at seeing this amazing sight.

I felt as if the waterfall had crashed over me, crushing me. It was the last straw somehow. To see something like this, alone, and with *them*.

The place here is tucked in under the overhang, below the road, where the land goes jaggedly down towards the ravines at the bottom of the cliff.

It was quite difficult, descending all those overgrown terraces. (They left the carriage and deer in a sort of shelter with the slaves, at the top.) Everything was slippery from blown spray.

Dragonflies drizzled through the spray-rain.

Then, we got here.

The building is built of the yellow stone, like the cliff, and again to start with I thought it was a natural rock, then I saw windows with glass, glinting.

It's just a low, square house, like something you'd find in Peshamba, maybe, but not so pretty.

In the courtyard H and Y started to act very picky and *Now we must do this the right way.*

No one seemed to be there, and then this woman came along the veranda above the steps. She looked like a servant, but she didn't bow or anything, just came up to us and stood there. I thought perhaps she wasn't used to visitors, out here, and hoped H and Y wouldn't get nasty with her.

'Is it one of those *things*?' asked Yazkool.

'Looks like it,' said Hrald.

Zand spoke in his language. Something about, 'Are the rooms ready for her?'

The servant nodded.

Her hair was odd. It didn't look like hair, more like tangled string.

When she spoke finally, in Zand's tongue, I realized.

'Click-click. Follow-click-me,' said she.

She's a mechanical doll, clockwork, like the guards and things at Peshamba. Rather rusty, as they weren't. Perhaps it's the damp.

All three servants here are the same.

The Peshamban dolls had seemed very efficient, and they'd looked good, but I never really got used to them in the short time I was there.

These ones made – *make* – me uncomfortable. I suppose because I'm usually dealing personally with them.

Y told me to follow the first one. (Nobody bothered to keep tabs on me, or warn me – where could I go?) It – well, she – led me to a suite of rooms, really one big chamber divided by bamboo or paper screens, or thin curtains. There was a bath, and she ran water into it. Hot and cold, from taps, just like the House and the City have. She also showed me a closet, and there were clothes in it. She said, 'Clickety-clok: Shall I bathe and dress you, clack?'

'Er – no thanks. That's great. I'll manage.'

'Shall I clunk clokkk?'

'Excuse me?'

'Clok: Bring refreshments?'

'Oh – that would be nice. Can I have some fresh drinking water?'

The food was basic on our journey, and the water had run out the last few days. You can get very tired of strong sweet sticky wine.

'Clum-clucky,' said the doll, and sailed out. (She walks in an odd way, a type of gliding *limp*.) (I still can't get over the urge to brush and comb her hair. Madness. Anyway it might all come out and then the poor thing would be bald.) (Her face isn't so bad, but expressionless. The eyes sometimes blink, startling me every time. Her lips part when she speaks, but sometimes only these clucks or cloks emerge.)

When she came back anyway, I'd had a fast nervous bath, not enjoying it as I'd have done normally. I'd put on a long loose dress from the row of long loose dresses, white or pale grey, in the closet. There were also some ankle boots of soft leather.

I rolled up my WD with this book still safe inside the pocket. (A Hulta Wedding Dress always has a pocket. The bride is given so many small gifts all through her wedding day, she has to have somewhere to put them.) I'd thought of that, too, got very down.

Then I shook myself. Just in time, for there was Dolly again.

On the tray she'd brought was a wonderful blush-and-cream fruit, some thin slices of a sort of crunchy bread, and a decanter and glass of green crystal. Cool water, as I'd asked.

'Thank you!' I cried.

She just went out.

Do you thank them? Does it matter?

Well, I do anyway. It feels wrong if I just snatch without a word, the way the other three do.

I didn't see *them* again until the evening. By then I'd slept a couple of hours on the low couch, a real deep, seemingly dreamless sleep. I felt better and stronger.

Dolly came into the room, clucked something about dinner on a terrace.

The view from my room's three high windows looks straight down into the jungle ravines, or up into leaf-fringed sky. Either way, mostly an impression of distance and things growing. A wild fig tree wraps the third window up almost entirely. So when Dolly led me up a short flight of stairs and I came out on a roof-terrace, the view made me dizzy again. All that largeness and space I'd seen earlier, but now we were perched right up inside it.

The sun was going down behind the house and jungle. Across from us, over the ravines, the cliff-face was burning hot gold, and the waterfall like golden silver. And the sky was a spicy colour. Overpowering.

Not taking any notice, Y, H and Z were sprawled about, smoking beetles.

Then we had dinner served by all three dolls, Dolly, and

two male dolls I've since called Bow and Whirr. Not very clever, I admit. Bow talks, but keeps bowing, and Whirr – just *whirrs*.

Dinner was all right, quite tasty, lots of fresh veg, fruit and salads, and some hot rice and pastry. No meat or cheese, or anything like that.

Hrald complained. 'Can't they get fish, even? There's a river down there, isn't there? Under that waterfall? Bad management. All this way, and not even milk for the tea.'

I didn't take much notice of them. They ignored me.

The sky was a smoked rose, then suddenly ash–blue. Stars starred it.

Then something *strange* – stars – gems – in the wrong place – at first I thought I was seeing things. Blinked, saw I wasn't.

I couldn't keep quiet.

'Over there – *what's that?*'

'What? Oh *that*. Hmm. What do you think?'

I scowled at Yazkool. 'If I thought I knew I wouldn't ask.'

'Oh, Claidissa, you're so loud and argumentative, so unfeminine –'

It was Zand who broke in. Gravely he told me, in my own language, 'The palace is there, madam.'

'Palace – that's a palace?'

The top of the huge cliff – I'd noticed in the last of the sun how it was all different shapes, especially along the top. I'd thought that was just how it had weathered. I've seen mountains, hills, shaped like towers or clumps of roofs. And this was all in the same stone . . . But now in the sudden dusk, spangles had fired up everywhere, up and down the entire cliff. They were gold and white, delicate lettuce green and ruby, amethyst . . .

Windows.

'It's called the Rise,' said Hrald. 'Didn't we say?'

Those beasts, of course they hadn't.

So the cliff is called the Rise. It runs for miles, up and down and along. And it's not a cliff, or not only a cliff. Not a palace either – it must be a city. And it's occupied, because all those windows were gleaming and blazing now in the dark, from lighted lamps. Like they do over there every night I've been here.

I sat feeling completely astonished. I was frightened too. Everything was too large. Nothing was properly explained. Perhaps it couldn't be.

But I wouldn't say anything else.

In the deep hollow of evening, far off yet weirdly clear, something growled, above the thunder of the fall.

'Tigapard, out hunting,' said glib Yazkool, knowingly.

'Or tiger,' added Hrald.

Zand shook his head. He said, still in my language, 'There are other things, on the Rise.'

And then – and then, to cap it all, as if too much hadn't already happened, this STAR rose over the cliff.

'My,' said Yazkool. Even he looked awed, for a moment.

Hrald just gawped.

Zand got up, jingling, and bowed even lower than Bow, to the Star.

Argul told me something about stars, the way some of them are suns of distant worlds, and some are nearer and are planets, worlds like ours, that wander through the skies by night. I've never quite understood, although I loved to hear him talk about it.

Is this a star, then? A planet? What? I don't know. Only that it's enormous. I mean I actually sort of measured it later. Holding up my hand, the Star up there, by then even higher, neatly vanished behind my thumb nail – but for its *glow*.

It's blue-white. It *gushes* light, dazzles. Stark shadows fall away from it over the ground, as if from a nearly-full moon.

Zand named it, in his own tongue. But I know what it's called now. I asked Dolly its name.

It's called the Wolf Star.

Well, that's all.

I mean, I've finished writing down the story of my kidnapping. Nothing else has happened.

We've been here three days and two nights. I've marked them on the top of a page in this book.

I stay in my room as much as I can. Some monkeys sometimes come and play in the fig tree, and I can watch them. They're noisy and funny. They throw fruit at each other, but sometimes they get violent, scream and beat their chests.

Every night, if I look, (I do look) the lights are lit in that cliff-palace over there, or whatever it is. And the great Star rises, gets higher, circles round somehow, is gone, comes *back*, and sinks. Did I ever see a star behave quite like that?

The Wolf Star.

The name isn't lost on me. No coincidence, it can't be. I don't know the link, though, Wolf Star and Wolf Tower.

Y and H are getting impatient, I can tell. Little things like the way they curse and stamp about and throw fruit all the time. (Though no screams or chest-beating.)

Everything has something to do with over *There*, probably.

Zand left the day after we arrived. I didn't see him go.

Why was he so polite that time he spoke to me?

I'm a prisoner.

Yes, I suppose I know something else will happen, to do with the cliff, the 'Rise'. But why should I think about it? I'm here, it's there. I can't see any way to cross, unless they or we fly.

Did think about running away again. Getting food from Dolly and putting it by, sneaking out by night. Surely cranky Whirr and Bow couldn't stop me? And if there are tigers and tigapards growling and roaring in the jungle and . . . 'other things', well, so what.

Maybe I will.

Tonight, maybe.

But anyway, I've done what I said I'd do, put all this down. I've written all I'm going to.

I have nothing else to say.

THERE

Today, I was sent over there. *There* is now where I am.

That other window was high. This one is HIGH.

The morning started with a bang. Literally. A monkey jumped in through the fig tree window, which I'd unluckily left open.

It landed on the tiled floor, day-edged and furry looking, but its eyes were like angry red coins.

Then its mouth pursed up and it kept going *Hwoup-hwoup* at me.

Obviously, I hadn't left in the night. I'd felt too tired, not ready – I was confused. (Cowardly.) Now I stood by the bed and the monkey stood about ten feet away going *hwoup* at me and showing its teeth in between, which I recalled Hrald had said, and even the Hulta had said, meant a monkey wasn't in a relaxed mood.

'Lovely monkey,' I gooed, creeping towards the door. 'Look, tasty mango in dishy. Have delishy mango-yum –'

But the monkey made a sudden leap and bounded up one of the curtains. I said they were thin, and the material tore and the monkey fell out of it, hit one of the paper screens, and screen and monkey went rolling about and now it was going *AargruffOOR!* at the top of its voice.

I ran out of the door and slammed it, and rushed up the steps to the terrace.

Dawn had happened about an hour ago behind the Rise. The sky was tall and full of birds.

Something was wrong with the terrace.

The table had been laid for breakfast, which looked started on, and Yazkool and Hrald's usual chairs were pulled out. But another chair lay on its side with a broken back. And there were three broken plates, and one of Yazkool's enamel beetle boxes – just lying there too, on the ground, open, with beetles and tobacco spilling out.

Monkeys were yammering from all the trees by the house.

Something had happened.

I yelled 'Dolly! Bow!'

Odd, really. H and Y were hardly my best friends, but I felt panicky.

For ages no one came. I heard the monkeys bashing about, and thought they might come up on the terrace and perhaps I should go back into the house. Then Dolly appeared and limped across to me.

'What's happened? Where are they? I mean Hrald, Yaz –'

'Clickups, clankit.'

'Oh *Dolly* –'

'Gone,' said Dolly.

'Yes, Dolly, but where – why?'

'Cluck: Duty done. Now you go to *Glack*!'

I nearly howled – and now here was Bow lurching up bowing and saying 'More juice, more toast!' And Whirr going '*Whirrr*' and I could hear the monkey in my room breaking more screens –

Then I saw the bridge.

I said we'd have to fly to reach the Rise. It wasn't necessary after all.

It was like a long white tongue that had licked out, a frog's or lizard's, from a little black mouth in the distant cliff-side. It had slid across the drop, through the spray of the fall, slid on and on until it touched and somehow attached itself into the rock on this side, and stiffened to stillness. By craning over the terrace, I could see the bridge's end, just by the courtyard wall.

'Someone came from over there,' I brilliantly guessed. 'By the bridge. And Yazkool and Hrald –'

'Away,' said Bow, bowing over his tray of excess toast.

'Do you mean *killed*?'

'Whirr,' said Whirr, thoughtfully.

This was useless. It would have been simple, presumably, for someone, or their guards or slaves, to hurl H and Y straight off this roof and away to the ravines below, to the jungle trees and the fish-river Hrald was always grumbling about.

Dolly was saying, 'Yack come over. You to go over cluck click.'

Me to go –

The bridge was for me to go – over –

Whirr was pushing at me. Was he trying to herd me to the bridge? Or worse – ? I tried to fight, and into my punching hands he thrust a piece of paper, folded once and with a seal of black wax.

I stared at it. For a minute the seal was all I could see. The wax had been stamped with the shape of – a wolf.

The dolls had all moved back, and now the monkeys were making less row. And like a fool I recalled, last thing last night, hearing Yazkool cursing away from the house stairs about dropping his second best beetle-box. So that had happened *then*, not because of some attack. As for the monkeys, the bridge would have scared them. Everything explained.

I broke the wax seal (it was a wolf with some sort of bird flying over it – ?) undid the paper.

The writing was in blackest ink, and the language of the House, and of Nemian's City, though some of the words were spelled another way; this didn't look like mistakes. It said: 'Greetings from the Rise. The men who brought you here have been paid and you may release them.' (Fine chance, they hadn't waited.) 'The bridge is for your convenience. Cross at your pleasure. The slave will escort you. Until we meet – *V.*'

That was all.

'What slave?' I nervously asked. The least important question.

Then anyway I saw him, standing waiting in the courtyard below. A man with thick green hair.

At the House, there were fashions and even rituals that involved differently coloured hair or wigs. At first I thought

43

the escort-slave was wearing a wig.

Before I left, I ate a mouthful of toast, swallowed a few sips of the green milkless tea. I had a bath and put on another dress. I brushed my hair. All this to waste time, to put off going. Also to see if it would be allowed.

Apparently it was. No one came to hurry me.

When I came out in the yard, the slave was still waiting, still just standing there, as if he hadn't moved an inch.

He wasn't mechanical. I kept wondering if he was. He was . . . odd.

I carried my WD and this book and pen, and a few things, underclothes, comb etc: in a bag I'd handily found in the closet. Put there to be handy for me?

Dolly, Bow and Whirr stood in the veranda, as if waving me off. So I waved. They didn't wave back. Why would they?

It'd been no use asking any questions either.

As we walked down the uneven slope between the fig trees and palms, towards the white bridge, I tried questioning the slave.

'What's your name, please?'

Instant reply. 'Grembilard,' he said.

'I'm Claidi,' I said. At the House, or in the City, one didn't speak to slaves like this, but what the hell.

'Lady,' however promptly said the slave.

'No, *not* lady. Call me Claidi. Try it.'

'Lady Claidi.'

That sounded ridiculous. But I let it go. Wanted to move on. 'Who sent you for me?'

Then the slave said something I thought meant he *was* a doll, and his mechanism had gone funny, like Dolly's and Whirr's.

'Could you repeat that?'

He did. I realized he'd put *Prince* on the front too, both times.

Was it a name? I tried it hesitantly over:

'Prince – Venarion-yellow Kasmel –'

Obligingly Grembilard helped me.

'Prince Venaryonillarkaslemidorus.'

'oh.'

Then we came around a giant stand of blue blooms like lupins, (eight feet tall) and there was the bridge.

I'd felt nervous. Now I felt Nervous.

'Who is he?' I demanded, stopping.

The slave stopped. 'Prince Venaryonillarkaslemidorus.'

'Yes, I know, but –' Grembilard took my bag. I looked at it in his hands. Everything had been taken out of my hands.

The bridge was terrifying.

How it had anchored itself into the ground this side I couldn't make out, but the earth was all displaced. The bridge looked solid. Immoveable. It was straight as a ruler, as it spanned the tremendous gulf. It was white as icing on a cake, with a lace-delicate rail that would come, once I stepped on the bridge, to just above the height of my waist – not very high. And it was *narrow*. Only wide enough for us to go single file. The distance from here to *there* was about a mile.

He walked in front. I was just supposed to follow. I followed.

At first I was afraid to look anywhere but at Grembilard's back and peculiar, leafy hair. My legs shook. I could *feel* the distance rushing below, down and down.

But the bridge was if anything *horribly* solid. It didn't even vibrate from our footsteps or the roar of the fall. Which got louder as we went on, and everything was slick with moisture, and then in places dry where somehow the fine spray didn't come.

(The noise of the fall is always there, and I seem always to be hearing it suddenly for the first, as if I've only just noticed it, or it's only just started, like a vast tap turned on in the cliff. But that's *because* it's constant, you just forget to hear it most of the time, hear other things above, below, around it.)

I think we were about halfway across when I thought I *would* look down.

The thing *anyone* – you, for example – would have said *don't do*. But I kind of had to.

So I stopped and put my hands firmly on the little hand-rail. I looked straight out, then over.

For some moments I was simply so astonished I didn't feel anything but – astonishment.

If the way across is a mile, it must be three miles, four miles, down.

There *is* a river at the bottom, a tiny shiny dark blue worm, coming and going through veils of spray. The fall reaches it, growing slender as a pencil, and *detonates*. And the sides of the Rise, and of the other cliffs, cascade towards the river, green bunched curtains caught with flowers and pineapples and tree-limbs, where parakeets flash red. Then, above, is a sky so large that I could just float free and up to one of those bubbles of cloud –

And that was when my head seemed to fall off *upwards*, and I sat down bump on the bridge.

'I can't move,' I said. 'I *won't* move.'

Giddy and mindless, I thought fearfully of what Argul would do – scold me, pick me up, drag me, or just sit and hold my hand until I felt better.

How I wished he was there. I started to talk to him.

'I'll be all right in a minute, Argul.'

The slave stood over me, indifferent.

'His hair,' I said to the imagined Argul, '*isn't* hair. It's got leaves in it.'

My head cleared. I said to the slave quite sharply, 'Why are there leaves in your hair, Grembilard?'

'They grow in it,' he said.

I felt sensible, nodded, and stood up. I was all right after that. I kept asking questions about his hair.

He answered them all, but we – I – got nowhere.

He says his hair is partly hair and partly leaves. Has to be washed and then watered, or something. It looks *real*. Couldn't be.

But I was all right.

I started to notice the cliff, the Rise, when we were about an eighth of a mile off from it.

It truly is enormous, and it does look natural, most of it, but every so often there is a part that, close to, you can see is carved out – a balcony or a bulging upper storey, long ranks of windows, with glass or lattices. Steps too, appearing and angling round, and towers, these with roofs of tiles but they're almost all faded, just a wink of indigo or lime here and there.

Masses of vines grow up the face of the rock-walls, and trees thrust out of them, as I'd seen from the other side.

Where the waterfall water*fell*, all I could see was spray like smoke, with a glitter of sun like dancing coins. But the fall itself was about three miles away along the cliff to my left.

Where the bridge had come out wasn't a hole, but a huge gatemouth.

47

We got nearer and I began to dread the gatemouth more than I'd dreaded the bridge.

But I couldn't really stop to admire the view again, so I went on.

Some pink parrots flew over as we got there. Then we were simply off the bridge and standing on another terrace. Cut stairs led up into the dim cavern or hall or whatever.

If I go in, will I ever get out?

And then I thought, Oh, come on. I've got out of everything else!

So I marched behind leafy Grembilard, up these old sloping stairs, and into the Mouth of the Rise.

WHERE?

What I said to him, to Argul, all that time – only a month or so – ago, about how the ring he gave me felt like a part of my hand. It does, so much so that I forget I have it on half the time, and in the beginning I sometimes knocked it on things.

The stone (diamond) is part cut and part polished. It's like a great tear.

I mention this now because it's all I have left of Argul. And because of what the slave said, Grembilard, as we walked into the cavern.

'Lady Claidi, I must ask, is that your mother's ring?'

My *mother*. I hadn't thought of her for a while. I mean, I'd never been sure what I was told about her was true – that she was called Twilight Star, was a princess, and so on. The story of my mother was one of the things that made me escape from the House with Nemian, and go to the City of the Wolf Tower. So it was told me, no doubt, to help make me do just that. On the other hand, *I* told Ironel Novendot the ring was my mother's, so I could wear it openly in the Tower. Ironel was the *only* one I told.

'Who told you that?' I asked Grembilard.

But all I got was 'The Prince —' (and that *name* again) 'may like to know if that is the ring of Twilight Star.'

'Then he can have fun guessing, can't he.'

But did all this really mean Ironel had sent word here, to this prince with a name of — what was it? — *eleven* syllables. Then that meant too she'd known I would be brought *here*?!

I looked round briskly. The cavern-hall was several storeys high, the ceiling rock carved with flowerlets and wiggles. The floor was old stone, polished with wear in places, and damp and going mossy.

Anyway, *why* did they want to know about the ring?

'Why does he want to know about the ring?'

'It has properties.'

'Like what?'

But only slavey silence now, and I was (slavishly) following him on, up another staircase, which had carved marble animals either side, tigers with beards, and things like bears.

Didn't matter did it, anyway. It *wasn't* Twilight's ring. If I was even her daughter.

A door opened to one side, straight off the stair. It opened I suppose by clockwork, since we didn't touch it and no one else was there.

He went in. I went in. The door shut.

There were lots of corridors after that, some quite narrow and others wide. Carvings, tiles, and here and there water dripping down the wall.

All the corridors had windows, some very high up so only sky was visible. In one wide corridor was a line of ten windows, floor to ceiling, about two man-heights high. They were of rich stained glass in complicated patterns. I must have seen them when I was across the gulf, once they were lit up at night. From this side you couldn't see through.

Sometimes there were closed doors, or other passages, arches, stairways.

I kept expecting to meet other people. There must be hundreds, thousands, in this palace-city inside the cliff.

We met no one.

That seemed – not right.

Once there was a very odd noise, a kind of grating rumble.

I said, 'What's that noise?'

Grembilard said, 'Just the palace.'

'Is it unsafe?'

He didn't answer. After that I kept thinking I'd see and feel galleries shaking or wobbly stones or plaster falling off the walls. But mostly the whole place seems in goodish repair. Even the water spills have only grown some attractive indoor mosses and ferns.

Anyhow, the sound died away.

We must have walked for about twenty minutes. Then he opened a door.

He handed me my bag. 'Here are rooms where you can stay,' said Grembilard. 'For now,' he added. (Ominously?)

These rooms are high, and pale banana yellow. There are three – no, four.

I sit in them or pace around.

Again, few furnishings. Low couches, a table or two, some fruit, water and wine, a sunken bath-tub – hot and cold water – a jar of some essence on the side, towels laid ready.

No *doors* in these rooms. Only curtains to screen the doorways.

And nobody about. Grembilard, having bowed me in, had bowed out, and I'd said anxiously, 'Where are you going? Now what happens?'

And he shrugged with a long face. 'Who can say?'

'What do you mean? When will I meet this Prince Venaridory-whatever?'

'Perhaps, soon. Or later. Whatever else, madam, please don't leave the rooms.'

'Well I thought you'd no doubt lock me in.'

'No. Unless you'd prefer it?'

'No I *wouldn't*! I might like another stroll.'

'Lady Claidi,' said Grembilard, 'there are . . . certain dangers in the palace – for this reason you shouldn't go outside the door.'

'Oh. I won't then,' I airily replied.

When he'd gone and I'd wandered around a bit, I did go and try to open the outer door to the corridors. And it did open.

What dangers? Do tigers and panthers run wild through the passageways?

Nothing out there – but then I heard that odd rumbling again. What was it? This time there was a definite vibration through the wall.

So I came back in.

I eventually noticed some of the fruit in the onyx dish has gone rotten.

Most of the windows in here have panes of milky non-see-through glass. They could face out on to anything – even other rooms.

Then I found *this* window, behind a gauzy curtain I'd thought was just a drapery.

Clear glass. You can look straight down and down to the

blue slow-worm of river.

Sitting by this window, I've written everything up.

What can I say. The most – well, it's –

Did I go to sleep and dream it?

No, because *she's* still there, the girl slave, sitting all innocent and cross-legged on the floor.

And the cat's here too, somewhere.

Sorry – that's confusing. What happened was this:

I got bored sitting. I had a bright idea. Since I'd found the window behind a curtain, there might be other things behind other gauzes hanging decoratively down the walls.

Not much to start. A mirror was behind one, and I saw myself and frowned hard at me. I looked changed and not myself. Behind another curtain was a door, an actual door made of wood and painted like the walls. I tried it but couldn't make it open. Left it, feeling irritated.

In the fourth room there was a cupboard behind a gauze with gold threads. In the cupboard I found piles of books, all in other languages and without pictures. Some did have maps, which made no sense to me. I wouldn't expect them to, never having been educated at the House.

The last gauze was also in the fourth room, and when I dragged it aside I found another door. Another cupboard, I thought, as I easily pulled it wide. It wasn't.

Outside was a vast hall of echoing stone. Granite pillars soared up, smooth as glass, and there was a great marble stair. Light streamed in at a round ceiling-window, a sky-light. It was high above, and through it I could see faint chalkings of cloud.

On the stair was this girl, with short black hair, sitting

crying her eyes out.

I said, idiotically, 'Are you all right?'

And I took a step out of the doorway –

What happened?

It's hard to describe it, really.

It was like being on that ship again, and like getting off the ship for the first hour or so, when the ground seemed to be moving as the deck had.

Everything *lurched*. I nearly fell flat, and then I did, but the other way, backwards, because the girl came hurtling off the stair and jumped at me. We tumbled into the room and got wrapped up in the curtain, which tore right off the wall.

The floor hit me in the back and the girl had landed on my stomach. Luckily she wasn't very heavy. As I lay there, gasping, saying things I usually try not to, I saw this:

Midway up, the stairway separated.

The top part then flew slowly up into the ceiling, and when it was almost at the sky-light, a large area of wall glided away, and the stair slid through. Then, from somewhere else – the other wall, only I hadn't seen it start – came what looked like half of a room, with a fountain in it in a stone bowl, trickling away. And this wheeled past and filled in the space between the door and the now-in-half stair.

Then everything stopped.

I couldn't see the pillars or the stairway any more. I couldn't see the sky-light. This other room, which now looked like a whole room, had fitted on to *my* rooms.

The girl had rolled away, and I sat up, and I stared. Then I too got up. And I was just going to go out into this sudden new room with a fountain, had one foot over the threshold, when the girl jumped me again and grabbed both of my arms.

I tried to push her off.

She shook her head so violently I thought it might come loose. She'd stopped crying. She had been streaming tears, but her eyes weren't even red. After we'd struggled a while, I snapped, 'All right. You don't want me to go in there. I won't.'

She let me go at once.

What was in this new room? Just the fountain. It was shaped like a big fish, quite elegant.

Then something moved on the stone bowl. It sprang off and came bounding over and in at my doorway.

A stone-grey cat. The oddest-looking cat – flame-green eyes and this *different* forehead – but it shot past and rushed into my rooms and I don't know where it's hidden itself.

The girl just went over there, and sat on the floor, inside my doorway.

No tears. *Had* she been crying?

She doesn't speak or can't, or won't. I don't know which.

Apparently I'm not allowed to go away from in here. Deliberately I walked to the outer door, and when I got there she came tearing after me. So I came back, and at once she sat down again.

Wait. I'll try asking –

I did. I said, 'Can you speak?' and she shook her head.

I said, 'Is it dangerous for me to go outside?'

Vigorous nods. Her neck must be really supple from all that urgent nodding.

I said, 'The stair – part of it moved – did it?'

To that, almost a *lazy* nod.

Then, this totally absurd thing.

She opened her eyes wide as wide, and streams, rivers of tears rushed from them. She had no expression. She didn't look upset.

When about two pails-full of water had poured on the floor, the tears ended. She got up and stood in the wet. Then she hopped and jumped about the room, like a kid playing, making wet footprints, (wet from her own *tears*) looking at them – and silently giggling.

She did this for a quarter of an hour.

Now she's sat down again.

As for the cat, I just saw it. It's in the fruit dish in room two. It's eaten every grape, orange and peach, and even the rotted mango. Now it's just sitting in the dish, washing itself nice and sticky. (Its head is shaped like – well, it's – ?)

Claidi, you need to make a plan.

Any plan.

No, I haven't, didn't.

Instead, this room –

Moved.

No, I didn't imagine it. Very loud rumbling started, and the floor jumped and shook for about two minutes. Next, when I looked out of the door to the passages, everything was different. There's a courtyard out there now, with roses and vines growing from pots. At the other door, which I'd left open, the room with the fountain is still there. It obviously came with us.

Probably the Tear Girl would have stopped me if I'd tried, but I didn't try, to go out by either way.

Something else has happened. The rooms became dark after we'd moved. I think the windows, though I can't see through, don't look out any more. Certainly the clear glass window doesn't. It now looks at a tall side of the cliff, where there are windows too, but also a looming cedar tree hangs over. (I noticed the Tear Girl did now appear rather worried.)

After it had been gloomy and dark for about five minutes, and I was wondering if there were any candles or lamps, *lights came on.*

That's the only way I can put it. Think of about fifty candles lit and burning up at once. Only steady, not flickery. And no one *lit* them.

The source of the light seems to be some of the carving at the tops of the four rooms.

I mean, this light is perfect, soft but clear. But how – what is it?

I've heard them – the House, the Hulta – talk about magic. Is this magic?

Before, I was scared, but I got used to being scared. It wasn't too bad. Now I'm frightened. It isn't even that. I'm – really lost. *Where* on earth have I come to?

These rooms haven't moved again. But I keep thinking they will. The lights burn steadily. Nothing's happened for about three hours, except that cat's gone to sleep in the fruit dish. Oh this is awful.

Obviously at last I decided I *was* going to leave the rooms. I couldn't stand this any more. I said to the girl, 'I'm just going to have a quick look outside . . .' I meant to make a dash for it. Though a dash to where or what I hadn't a clue.

I put my bag casually over my shoulder by its carrying strap, walked about, walked to the door, yawned and stretched.

She didn't seem agitated . . . I'd fooled her?

Really, it was quite an attractive yard. The roses were scented and twined round pillars. There was a grapevine heavy with fruit.

Tall windowless walls enclosed the court above. At the top was sky. It seemed very dense and blue – afternoon? I'd probably been here longer than I thought.

Was there another way out?

I'd delayed too long being casual. Here was Tearful at my side. The cat had woken up and come too, smelling strongly of peaches. What it was with its head was that the area between the ears was too thick and high – its ears looked tiny, but weren't. Its eyes though were enormous.

'Isn't that a strange cat?' I said to Tearful.

Then I broke into a sprint.

Oh they both shot after me, Tearful with her thin arms out to clutch, and just missing me, and the cat with its little ears laid flat on its big domed forehead.

Luckily there was an archway behind the vines. I belted straight through, (with the bag thumping me on the back as if to hurry me up) and as I did so I heard something start creakily to *move* behind me, and felt the ground *sway*. But I just pelted on. (Once I also felt Tearful's clawy fingers catch my hair, but I managed to rip it free.)

I don't think I ran *that* far.

There were more corridors and courts and hallways, and now and then more stairs. We were deep inside the cliff, I thought, for at no point did I recognize the outer wall of it, and although there were coloured windows in places, they seemed to look into rooms, not out at the gulf. Towers piled above.

In darker corners, and behind some windows, there was this light burning, often from a source I didn't even see. Twice I ran under a great lit hanging lamp – the glow in both of them was as steady as if the light had gone *hard*.

Of course I didn't know where I was going, and anyway I got tired. I was emptily hungry too, painfully dry – and scared, fed-up.

Suddenly in front of me reared an arch with a gate of curly wrought iron.

Not able to stop, I ran right into it and it swung gently open.

I burst through on to a broad path laid with bleached gravel.

And then I couldn't run any more. I was bent almost double crowing for breath. I had a stitch, too.

The pumping of blood in my head made everything zoom in and out. When that went off, I saw I'd come into what looked like a formal, exotic park.

Behind and to either side was the cliff/palace. And far over there, through a cloud of trees, some other tall rocks-or-buildings going up, one with a golden globe on its top, blinding back the afternoon sun. The rest was sloping lawns, blooming shrubs, twenty-foot bamboos.

On the path behind me, by the gate, stood Tearful, also panting for breath. The cat had kept up too. (I think it had found cat short cuts, and jumped over things we'd had to run along.) Another cat, a brown one, now came to join it, also with a curious domed forehead. But they were soon having a completely ordinary cat fight, yowling and kicking and bashing through a rhododendron.

Then Grembilard walked out of some tulip trees.

'You're here, then, madam,' he said. I still couldn't speak. I scowled at him instead. 'If you'd stayed in the rooms it would have been easier,' he had the unbelievable sauce to say.

'For whom?' I had to croak.

'Everyone,' he patiently moaned.

'They *move*,' I accused. 'The rooms. The stairs —'

No reply. He was taking my bag again. I let go. We walked down the path, Grembilard at the front, then me, Tearful, and next the cats, falling in behind.

IN THE AIR-HARP GARDENS

There are fireflies in the gardens. Also nightingales. And the harp-things sometimes sing, too.

None of that is important. I'm sorry, maybe it is.

Maybe I'd better tell you about Venn.

I really must try to start at the beginning. All right:

Grembilard led me (us) across this park, which I've since been told is called the Air-Harp Gardens. I did notice jungly colossal trees, and pavilions (like at the House, but different.) There was a *little* waterfall that splashed down three or four terraces, to a pool. The thunder of the big fall was softer, away around the side of the Rise.

We reached a lawn with a statue of some sort of spread-winged heron. Here on a table was food, some of it under covers, and another slave – only he turned out to be another *doll* – waving insects and tiny little birds away from the plates and bottles.

'I thought you'd *never* get here,' he fussed, flapping round us. Though he was mechanical, all the parts of his face moved. He had *expressions*. 'Please, *do* sit down,' and he seated me, and Tearful, treating us both like royalty.

The lemonade had got warm and the boiled eggs were cold, but it wasn't bad.

It was a Tea. (Like the Teas Jizania had, at the House, for every meal.)

The doll – Grembilard calls him Jotto – fussed round all the time. He leapt to serve us all. He even let the cats on the table, and put plates for them, and spooned on eggs and toast and biscuits and butter, and chopped them all up to make them easier for the cats' teeth to get to. When he wasn't running up and down doing that, he was running up and down waving off the bees and dragonflies and humming-birds with a feather fan.

I felt tired when I'd eaten, but still very Nervous. Also, the sun was westering behind the rocks/buildings. The sky was that spicy colour it goes just before and just after sunset. Where had today gone?

'Oh, I do hope he'll be here soon,' fussed Jotto. He was nice, really, kind and wanting to help so much you wanted to slap him. But, I mean, he's clockwork! No doll I've ever come across (although I suppose my experience with them is limited) ever had a *personality*!

'He?' I demanded. 'Who?'

'Prince Venarionillarkasl –'

'Oh, him.'

'You see,' fussed Jotto, opening a jar of fruit and offering it to the grey cat, 'he knew it would take ages to find you, probably. But now he's probably having to do it *twice*, since you unfortunately left the first set of rooms.'

'I see,' I lied.

'Poor prince,' said Jotto rather cheekily – or not? They wouldn't have stood for that at the House. 'This place can be *such* a trial.'

I was surprised he thought so too. Surprised he *thought* anything.

'I don't understand about the rooms moving,' I announced flatly.

Jotto opened his mouth, then hesitated. 'I get a bit muddled.'

Grembilard said, 'Prince Ven–etc–etc: will explain.'

'Oh, yippee.'

The sun set. Grembilard scratched at his leafy hair and Tearful got up and went and cried on it, gallons. Grembilard rubbed the water into his scalp. 'Thank you, Treacle. That feels much better.' (He's not really like a slave, Grembilard.) And she's called Treacle.

Then, in the quick red afterglow, Jotto pointed excitedly.

'Look, there's his light!'

We looked. A tall yellow window had lit under the gold globe, in the rocks.

'Lights here just light anyway, don't they?' I said.

'Oh yes, lady dear,' said Jotto kindly. 'Only *his* is a special *oil* lamp. He does so like to be different.'

Oil lamps, like candles, are what I'm used to. I realize by now, it may not be the same for you.

But well, anyway, we got up and trooped off into the darkening trees, through the fireflies that were also lighting up, and after about ten minutes were under the rock-building, looking up about seventy feet at *his* window.

'Halloo! Halloo, prince!' yelled Jotto.

Grembilard made a kind of loud whooping noise. Treacle and the cats danced about.

I stood there like a total twit.

In the end, after an age, part of the lighted window opened.

A dark figure leaned out its head and shoulders.

'Yes? Is that you, Grem?'

Something about his voice – I didn't at once know what – made all the fine hair on my scalp and neck stand up.

A 'City' voice. A Wolf Tower voice.

Like *Nemian's*.

Pale moths flickered between us and him, attracted to his light.

'Shall we come up, prince?' cried Jotto.

'*No.*' *That* was definite. 'Wait. I'll come down.'

As the window shut, Jotto whispered to Grembilard, 'You don't think he was – *up* there all the time? I mean, I thought he was still *looking* for her.'

Grembilard said nothing.

I wanted to move back into the deepest shadows, but I stayed where I was. It *wasn't* Nemian, even if he'd sounded so like him.

No, he wasn't Nemian.

A stair curved down the rock-tower, and he came down that. He was carrying another lamp, which lit him up in a peculiar way, from one side and below.

He just looked like what he was, a stranger.

Then, when he was only about ten steps up, he paused, and looked over at us all, angling the lamp.

I thought, *He's short-sighted or something*.

He was peering at us.

And then, the way the light fell, suddenly it filled in his face properly, as if it hadn't been completely there before.

He's pale skinned and his hair, which is thick, falls to his shoulders, and is light brown and loosely curling. His eyes are black. That's the same. I mean, that's the same as the one he looks like. He looks like –

(I swallowed air the wrong way.

Jotto hit me on the back.

Treacle wriggled in a giggle without sound.)

Argul.

He looks like Argul.

No, he can't, he *can't*.

He does.

There was an eerie whining noise. I thought it was just something *I* was hearing. But Jotto waved up at this oval hoop with strings in a tree. A night breeze was passing, and made the strings 'sing', apparently. (It's very unmusical.) Then a monkey screamed somewhere. Stopped. 'The air-harps,' smirked Jotto. 'Clever, aren't they.'

Then a nightingale started.

I burst out madly laughing. Jotto looked startled: Should he thump me on the back again?

He just stood ten steps up. And now the angle of the lamp was different, and he didn't look like Argul, or not so much.

And the awful, horrible thing is – I wanted him to. Such a lot.

'That's late tonight,' he said, as the huge Star rose.

We were sitting on chairs G and J had brought, in the clearing under the rock-tower. Apparently, this building doesn't move, just as the gardens don't.

Starlight shattered through the trees and hit the grass like shards of broken glass.

'That Star is very large,' I said.

'Is it? Oh. Yes.'

He was uninterested. In the Star, in me, in everything. You could tell he was itching to get back into the tower, to be alone.

He'd sent the others off, in quite a friendly, relaxed way. When he turned to me, he was cool and distant.

The note he sent me read *Until we meet.* But it was now obvious he hadn't *wanted* to meet me. Either that or I was the most ghastly disappointment.

So – what was all this about?

'Prince Venari – er – Yill – er –' I tried.

'Call me Venn,' he said shortly.

'– Prince Venn, why am I here?'

'Oh why indeed,' he said, off-hand, gazing away through the trees. 'To be useful?'

'That's nice. In what way, and to whom?' (What excellent grammar! Didn't I dare not to speak properly, with *royalty*?)

'To me, perhaps.'

'I see. And how am I meant to do that?'

'Well, Claidis,' (*Claidis*, that was new) 'frankly I'm not at all sure. But there. You're doubtless a mine of information. You're like a book from the library. I shall want to consult you, I expect. One day.'

'About what?'

'All the things you know.'

'I don't know *anything*.'

He flicked me a glance iced with distaste. 'You're too modest.'

'I'm not modest, I'm telling you the truth. Who on earth do you think I am?'

He looked down his nose. He did it just as Argul does, when he's being – Argul. But this was – *Venn*.

'This is rather silly, isn't it?' he said.

'No. Or if it is, that's not my fault. Those men abducted me, dragged me here, and I want to know why, and saying I'm a mine of information is like saying – like saying *Treacle is chatty*.'

'I find all this rather dull,' he said. 'Don't you?'

I sat there, and my mouth dropped open, so I shut my mouth and I thought, I feel as if I'm going nuts.

He just looked away through the trees. Then he glanced at the Star, which was now directly above. How fast it climbed – was it always so fast? Just tonight? – or had we just sat here that long?

Then: 'I hope everything is comfortable for you, Claidis.'

'Of course it isn't!' I screeched.

He got up.

He's slightly taller than Argul, which of course makes him look too tall.

'Perhaps we should talk tomorrow,' he graciously said, 'or in a few days time.'

'Let's talk now.' I too got up. 'All right. I'm your prisoner. But I –'

He gave this soft blank laugh. As if I'd told a boring joke but he must be polite.

'Next month, then,' he said.

The night breezes twittered and whined in the non-musical air-harp strings. Monkeys bawled. And three or four nightingales chirruped as if they had hiccups.

'Wait,' I said. And I heard Argul, oddly, in my voice, his authority. And it stopped this man a minute. (How old is he? A year or so older than Argul, probably. But he's like a man *much* older, *fifty*, say. Set like cold cement.)

'Wait for what, madam?'

'Why are you calling me that? I'm a slave, aren't I? You don't say *Madam* to a slave. I was brought here and I don't know a thing about anything – about the world – or about this place. I don't even know where I'm going to have to sleep.'

'Grembilard will,' he said, 'naturally find you a suitable

chamber. *If* you stay put this time, it will almost certainly not move. Of course, I can't guarantee it, the palace being what it is.'

'This palace is *insane*!' I shouted.

'True. It was made to be mad, by my mother. One of her most cunning tricks.'

The Star blared on the clearing. His face was blue-white. I expect mine was too.

Then something growled, long and low, echoing and seeming not far off.

'It's only a vrabburr,' he chillily (I think) said.

'Oh, *that's* all right then.'

'They don't come into the gardens. Stay inside the walls and you'll be perfectly safe.'

'Oh will I? *Will* I?'

'I'm afraid, Claidis, I don't understand you,' he said. 'If it's all been so difficult, you shouldn't have asked to come here, should you?'

'ASKED???' That was all I could get out.

Somewhere or other, the safely-outside vrabburr, (or another one) growled again. Which was the only reply I got.

Venn–etc: just walked off. He was on his stair, going up, back to his room.

From the back, he didn't look like Argul, or Nemian – or anyone I'd ever met.

I sat down again on my chair; I was so stunned I didn't even try to think.

After a while Jotto appeared. He bent over me.

'Don't you fret, now,' said Jotto. 'He can be a bit – stand-offish. His mother, you know. She was very harsh. Left him when he was only nine. Grem says the Rose Room will be all right. Come and see.'

The west walls, which face across the gulf west, and the outer corridors there, and most of the rooms in these outer areas of the Rise, don't move ever. That is, they don't have the mechanisms and can't.

It seems my yellow rooms, though in the west wall, do move – well, they did. But they hadn't for 'years', and were thought 'quiet'.

The inner rooms of the palace can almost *all* move. They do it at will – only it isn't will – it's some clockwork thing, which makes them shift about, sliding and slotting around each other, but not in any real order.

Although Jotto told me that some rooms and sets of rooms do tend to 'go wandering off' about the same times of day and night, and in the same sort of direction – 'quite often'.

He started explaining all this, or trying to, as he showed me the Rose Room. He was obviously trying to cheer me up, console me for Venn-etc: being unfriendly. But it just added to my feelings of utter furious frantic bewilderment.

'The thing is, you mustn't go out of here until we fetch you. Someone will always come to *you*, if you press this carved flower, here. They may take a little while, though, so be patient, lady dear. Sometimes a walk of ten minutes can take all *morning*, the way things move around.'

Apparently if a human presence – or even a clockwork one, as Jotto bashfully added – is in a room, it doesn't normally move but stays put.

Treacle had been left in the yellow rooms earlier, just in case, to keep them anchored. She only slipped out when I came in. Then, when I put one foot outside, (twice) the yellow rooms 'woke up'. Perhaps they thought I'd gone. Anyway, they got frisky. (That was why Treacle had tried to stop me going out and jumped right at me.) After that though, even when she and I stayed in the rooms, they took off. And the staircase had moved, hadn't it, too, when Treacle left it.

Was I even listening to Jotto's explanation? I must have been, to be able to write it down now. Does it make any sense? I doubt it.

Finally I said to Jotto, who was by then artistically arranging some pineapples he'd collected on the way, in a dish, 'Who told Ve – *him* – I *asked* to come here?'

Jotto glanced at me. 'Well. I can't say. Your companions, perhaps?'

'That Yazkool, you mean, and Hrald – ?'

'Or it might have been in the flying letter.'

'The – what's that?'

'Oh, just a letter, dear.' Intent on getting the last pineapple *just* right, Jotto held up his hand for silence.

'Oh blast the pineapples, Jotto. He has to be told – *now* – that I was brought here against my will. And I – want to go home!' I added in a wail.

But Jotto just positioned the last of the fruits and beamed at me. 'There, isn't that better? Nothing like a proper display of fruit and flowers to make things civilized. Now don't you worry. You'll feel right as rain after a nice sleep.'

'You don't believe me. *He* didn't. Of course I'd *have* to want to come here,' I sarcastically added.

'That's *right*!' cried Jotto, even his beam beaming.

I gave up.

This Rose Room is about twenty feet tall. Everything is roses, and rose colour, including dresses in its closet. I hate it, naturally.

VRABBURRS AND OTHERS

I suppose another endless century has gone by. Haven't marked the days or anything. Days here are alike, and even weather seldom changes, except for a couple of insane storms. (You can see them *coming*, from the Rise.) I've counted twenty cats, all with domed foreheads. But since a lot are black or brown, and I haven't seen all of them up close, some might be ones I'd already counted . . .

What to put down. I mean, things have sort of happened. Nothing much.

I'm supposed to stay in this big room, because it won't move about if I'm *in* here. And it hasn't. But I've been out too, into the gardens, which don't move ever, thank goodness.

I fully expected the Rose Room to have made off when I came back, and I'd taken everything I wanted outside with me. But the Room was there. Jotto says this R. Room is 'sleepy'. It hasn't gone anywhere for ages. (I reminded him about the yellow rooms, also said to be quiet, which hadn't been. He seems to think that's different.(?))

Anyway, the R.R. opens right on to the gardens, so it's convenient for that at any rate. (Oh, Jotto keeps chickens, by the way. I'd wondered where the eggs came from.)

Lights come on in the lamps in here at sunset. The lamps are closed rosy glass roses, so I can't see what makes the light, which doesn't flicker, and goes out when I lie down on the bed. (The first time that happened I jumped up again and at once the light returned.)

It's the old thing, isn't it. This whole foul business *is* an Adventure. I should be energetically exploring, making notes.

The more I find out, after all, the more chance I have of learning how to get away from here and back to – Argul. Somehow that was difficult to write. It's as if I've totally lost him. As if – I'd ceased to exist in Argul's world. I can't explain. But it's an awful feeling.

I *have* asked questions, of Grembilard, and Jotto, and of another one I call the Gardener, because I always find him in the gardens, neatly scything the lawns or re-stringing airharps. I'm pretty sure the Gardener is a doll, but he's even more realistic-looking than Jotto, and he's sullen and grunts at you like a bad-tempered slave. Maybe he *is* a slave?

Grembilard, though a slave, (the letter Venn sent told me he was) is obviously a favourite of Venn's. Twice I've seen them talking, all friendly and easy, in the distance. I never approached. The one time I came through a grove of strawberry trees, and there they were strolling along, Venn's *face*. He looked almost *afraid* at the horror of Claidi, her appallingness. He gave me a brisk nod, turned and stalked off.

One evening too, I saw a big pale bird floating over the gardens, and Jotto said, 'There's the prince's owl.'

He doesn't look so much like Argul. It was just that first time I saw him, somehow he truly did.

Well, he does, rather. Sometimes more than others.

Why does he?

All this is such a muddle, and I almost have this feeling they sent me on purpose to someone who looks like Argul, just to make things worse. But what would be the point of that? Then again, why tell him I wanted to be here?

And who are *They*, anyway?

Ironel? Jizania? The Wolf Tower?

Questions I've asked, where I got no sense out of anyone here, are these:

1) Why am I here?

2) When can I leave?

3) Why did Venn's mother make the palace-cliff move about inside?

4) Who was Venn's mother? (Grembilard did say her name but I can't remember it.) (Uzzy-something.)

5) Why did she go and *where* did she go? (Into the jungle, said Grem. That was all.)

6) What makes the hard still lamplight? (The waterfall said Jotto, on that occasion.) So,

7) How? (Jotto couldn't say. Grem couldn't or wouldn't. Didn't even bother to ask the Gardener, and of course not Treacle.)

8) When can I talk to Venn properly? By which I mean I'll make an appointment. (I dread this, but it's necessary. I have to convince him somehow. He dislikes my being here so much, *evidently*, he might help me to go?)

9) What *scrowth-cha-chaari* is? (The Gardener shouted this at three cats who were clawing some trees. Probably it's not polite. Jotto went very vague when I asked him.)

Bits of information I've received are these:

a) I should just 'enjoy my stay' here!!! (Jotto said this. You guessed? He hasn't taken it in, and won't, (like all of them) that I'm a PRISONER.)

b) That Grem set out from the gardens to fetch me from the other side of the gulf *two days* before he reached the outer corridors and could operate the bridge. This was because of the rooms and stairs and halls and so on all moving extra weirdly.

c) (And this may be interesting?) The cats here, which run about wild, all came from three cats originally brought here – when? With Uzzy-something? They haven't said –

71

and the cats were ordinary then. But they have, over the years, developed thick bone ridges on their skulls! (!) To protect them when architecture suddenly shifts and they bang into things. Should I believe this? It's the kind of story I never would have believed – if I hadn't seen the cats.

Actually, lots of things here are . . . altered, or have been very changed.

Grem, for example. Real leaves do grow in his hair, which is anyway more like grass. How on earth can that be? (I haven't asked him. It seems – rude.)

And Treacle. That crying-which-isn't. She comes in and waters the indoor roses in pots, streams gushing from her eyes. Then she does a pleased little dance. I *did* mention her 'tears' to Jotto. I said, 'How is it Treacle can cry like that?' Jotto said, enthusiastically, 'Yes, it's *brilliant*, isn't it?' 'No, but *how*?' 'Well don't ask *me*, dear,' said Jotto, as if thrilled to be ignorant.

He's always carrying on like that, but he's nice, too. And then again, look at *him* – he's mechanical – But.

Then there are those things that growl – vrabburrs – they don't sound right, either.

Argul, what would you do? It's almost as if I can't even see you mentally, in my mind, any more. How long is it since I was there with you, that morning in the Hulta camp? Months. For ever.

The Rose Room moved this morning. I was just getting out of bed, and almost fell over. It didn't go far, only round the back of some Lily Rooms or something, according to Jotto, who found me after a quarter of an hour.

Anyway, once I'd got dressed, I put my stuff in the bag and went out through the corridor which now led from the door, got into the gardens, and now I'm not going back.

He has rooms that don't move. If I'm stuck here, I too want a room that absolutely doesn't.

I've had enough of all this.

But late afternoon I hadn't done anything, hadn't seen anyone even. I *found* some lunch on a table, though I had to share it with six cats, some humming-birds and a bee, oh and a black-faced monkey that joined us halfway through. Food seems to get left out, here and there, I suppose by Jotto, who seems to do the cooking(?) Sometimes silver covers protect it, or else various animals knock them off.

All the lunching animals were quite unaggressive. In these gardens, they seem used to people or dolls. The cats ignored the humming-birds and bee in preference for the custard tart. (They don't seem to eat meat. No one does here. Maybe the cats have forgotten that birds are prey. But I'm not complaining.)

Later I found a wilder part of the gardens, and climbed up and down through flowering thickets, and came up on a ridge. I've found places like this before, here, but not one so high. From it I could see, not just for miles, but over half the world, it looked like.

This side of the palace, the Rise mostly falls down and down through cascades of trees, until the jungle-forest wholly reclaims it. Then the jungle pours away and away, green turning to turquoise, and so to blue where it finally melts into the sky.

Wonderful views, these, but disturbing too. The jungle really seems to have no end, no beginning now, either.

Then a storm started to build over there, in the great upturned bowl of the east.

Weather coming is always curious to watch from the Rise. With a storm, a sort of boiling starts on the horizon, then mountains of cloud block up.

The tops of the clouds, as they came massively and slowly tumbling towards the Rise, caught gold from the westering sun. The lower clouds were slatey-mauve. Lightning twitched inside them. But here the sky was clear.

It seemed to me I'd see all this better from the next ledge over. So I hefted my bag and climbed across through the stones and bushes, being careful not to tread on two sleeping snakes.

When I reached the next ledge, instead of looking at the gathering storm, I looked about and along. There was a wall there, which I hadn't seen earlier for trees and bushes. It was an old wall, but sturdy, about ten feet high. And there was a gate in it, old warped wood, braced with iron.

I thought, as the thunder-light stabbed nearer and nearer, I've got all my things. I've got a peach and some cheese and a cake left over from lunch. I thought, Well, should I try? There's a gate, there might be another road. And somewhere is the sea. There are other people, villages surely, towns, ships, chances.

Such a lot of time seemed just to have dripped away. Suddenly I was crazy.

When I got to the gate, the distant thunder was starting to sound loud, as if the storm might mean something, wasn't just fireworks in the sky.

The afternoon went copper.

There was a ring-handle in the door. *It will be locked* I thought – *or stiff from disuse*. I'd find a stone and bash it open.

But the handle turned easily, recently oiled, and the door parted from the wall and there was a pale glimmering path going away and down, between tall trees.

I didn't pause. I just walked out of the gate, turning only to push it back flush with the wall.

Under the trees it was dark, but the path did seem to glow.

The air felt electric from the storm. Shadows massed against and through everything. Eyeholes of metallic sky winked with lightning.

It came to me, Venn saying in his unbearable way, *Stay inside the walls and you'll be perfectly safe*.

Stay in this room, in that room. Stay inside the walls. *Stay inside the rules*.

The path swerved and as I followed the coil of it, from a stand of eucalyptus, a beast came out.

In books, I've read about being turned to stone, or ice. I *had* been.

There were lions at the House, I've said. And I've seen other animals. I've even seen pictures of tigers, somewhere.

This wasn't – it was –

Sorry.

What was in front of me was a tiger. That is –

It was big, about twelve feet long, if it had been standing on all four legs. It wasn't though. Which was because its back legs were much heftier, and the front ones were smaller, and it held those up against its chest. It was tawny, and barred by black stripes – almost like a zebra – the way tigers are. Its underbelly was a creamier colour, and all the fur was short, like well-brushed plush.

The head was more like a dog's face than a cat's. But it *was* a cat's, and from the mouth these huge canine teeth, white as peeled nuts, stretched out and over the lower jaw. It had little piercing brilliant eyes. They were palest blue.

Tiger's ears are small and rounded, almost toy-like, I do remember that. These ears were tall. They were tawny and had paler fur inside. They had stripes. But they were the ears – of a gigantic rabbit. It was – a *rabbit*. A rabbit with a dog-cat's face and the skin of a tiger, and prehistoric teeth for serious rending.

And it wasn't funny. You couldn't laugh at it.

It was terrifying.

Then it growled. The sound went right through me, and I started to shake. Everything else seemed to, too. The leaves were shaking – no, it was a spatter of rain coming down.

That was jolly. It would rain while this rabbit killed and ate me.

You could tell it wasn't non-meat-eating, like the Rise cats. You could *tell*.

It dropped its top legs/arms down, and it was on all fours. This pushed its back end upwards, and its head craned up to look at me on a too-long neck.

When it sprang it looked just like a big cat springing, but like a rabbit as well, you know, when they bound.

You see, I was just rooted there, watching this monstrous thing, plunging through the air at me. Where it landed would be where I stood. It would land *on* me, perhaps just breaking me instantly in two. That would save it some time.

God (that is a prayer, I think) God knows, I didn't have any thoughts. I just thought in a scream. Though I couldn't scream aloud.

And then the tiger-rabbit came down and it wasn't on me, but about a yard away in a clump of hibiscus.

Cats play with their prey. Was this playing with me?

It was crouched there, on all fours. Its eyes glittered and its mouth was redly open. I missed something – its tail would be wagging – wouldn't it? But then, did it have a tail? If so, which sort – long and barred like a tiger's, or a powder-puff thing like a rabbit's?

Venn walked on to the path.

I said, 'What tail does it have?'

'I beg your pardon?'

'Its t-t-t-tai-lll –' suddenly I couldn't speak. I found I'd sat down, quite gracefully, on the path.

Venn made that *tstch* sound elderly people sometimes do when they're annoyed with you.

Thunder and lightning collided overhead.

In the flash I thought the rabbit-tiger moved – but it didn't. The jungle went luminously black and again rain crackled through.

'Why isn't it?' I said. I could speak after all.

'What?'

What? Did I know what I was saying?

'Why isn't it killing me? Has it . . . got bored?'

But I could just make him out, moving through the harp-strings of the rain, bending over – it.

'I did tell you,' said Venn, with cold reasonableness.

'To stay in the gardens,' I said. I said, 'Is that – a vrabburr?'

'Yes.'

I got up. The rain felt wonderful. The point was, I hadn't thought I'd still be alive to feel it. Coming over to the hibiscus, I looked and saw the vrabburr had a tail. It was a tiger's tail, long as a bell-rope, but tufted with a black rabbit's puffball.

What was Venn doing? He was squeezing the vrabburr's right forepaw. Shaking hands?

'You were exceedingly lucky,' said Venn.

'Hurrah.'

It didn't have any smell, the vrabburr. And it was beautifully clean and tidy, even crouched there in the rain.

'It's a doll,' I said.

'In a way.'

I started to sing a happy song from long ago. Realized and shut up.

'You're hysterical,' he remarked. Hysterical Claidi, how tiresome for him.

'Oh – *scrowth-cha-chaari*!' I shouted.

'That doesn't seem likely.'

'Why not?'

'I don't eat much fur,' he said. He went on squeezing the vrabburr's paw. I'd realized, this must be like turning a sort of key, to wind it up, but nothing was happening. Oh, it was my fault, no doubt. I'd ruined it by somehow not letting it tear me to pieces. Venn stood back. His curly hair was flattened and black in the dark rain.

I said, 'What does *scrowth-cha-chaari* mean?'

'May you get fur-balls.'

The vrabburr blinked.

'It's all right now,' he said, as if I *cared*. 'We have about three minutes before it starts up again. You'd better come with me.'

Humbly I trudged after him, off the path, through the dripping boughs and vines.

'You often come out here?' *Why* was I trying to make conversation.

'Now and then. I don't go far.'

'Are they clockwork?' I asked.

'What? The vrabburrs? No, not all. That's why you were so lucky.'

Lucky me.

Presently – it was almost black as night, blacker, without the Wolf Star – we came up against a bank. Rock, ferns, bamboos, a door. Door?

Venn did something to the door, it opened, and he went into the rockside. I, of course, followed. I sometimes wonder what is the matter with me. But at least we were out of the rain and horror-rabbit range.

It was a tunnel, lit by some other sort of magical light. Otherwise, it was a bit like the tunnels that led around from the House through the Garden. Like the one I used to escape through, with Nemian, which also went out under a wall.

Then, a hollow with an ironwork gate. I recognized it.

'You have lifters, like in the City.'

'Lifts? Oh, yes.'

He stood back gallantly to let me go in. I'd always hated the lifters in the Wolf Tower. I didn't like this one either. It was very bumpy.

Up and up we bumped. I thought, Oh, we're going up into his rock-tower, under the gold globe, where he has that so original oil lamp. I *am* honoured.

I was right, too. When the lift-lifter arrived, we stepped out into this eight-sided room lined with books, and with dark old polished chairs and a table, and a stair going up into a high dome with a round glass window looking like half a cut orange. The sky looked orange through the glass, too. And I could see part of the gold globe that sits on top of the rock.

It reminded me slightly of the black wolf statue on the Wolf Tower.

He was towelling his hair with a cloth. There was no light but the orange storm-light. He didn't look like Argul, or Nemian, or anyone. He looked like a young man who'd got rained on.

There was a wine-red rug. I stood and dripped on it.

Lots of books. And some little enamel figures. And a bird – I hadn't noticed it before – the white owl, on a perch, snoozing near the window with the famous lamp.

I have to admit, it was a good room. Interesting and lived-in. Comfortable, which surprised me. Not comfortable for me, of course.

'Oh, have this,' he grudgingly said, handing me another mop-up cloth.

But it was warm, even at night it's never worse than cool. My hair was already drying.

Above, around, the storm crackled and flicked its tawny vrabburr tail.

'I suppose you'll want tea, or a cordial.'

'Will I.'

'At least you haven't fainted away,' he disgustedly added.

This was the sort of thing that happened with Nemian, all over again. This fool thought I was *sensitive*, a lady, royalty. Claidis.

'Listen,' I said, 'it's time we got a few things straight.'

He gave me that look again, *scared* of my time-wasting and annoyance-potential. He sat down in a big chair quite a long way off.

'All right. Let's get it over with.'

I took a deep breath. 'Someone you think is important obviously told you I wanted to come here, and they told you too I was royal, called Claidissa or Claidis. You loathed the idea but couldn't say No.'

'That's about right, yes.'

'However,' I said, 'I'm not royal. Or if I am, only half, and anyway that may all be a lie. Let me tell you my story – oh, I'll be really quick, don't worry. It's soon said. I grew up in

80

a place called the House, which you may have heard of.'

'Yes.'

'Good. Then you may have an idea what it's like there. Slaves, in the House, or in the City on the River, are rubbish. And I was just one step up from a slave, a maid-servant. Well, I left the House, helping a man called Nemian escape back to his City tower, the Wolf Tower. Heard of that too? Thought so. For some reason I still don't properly grasp, they wanted *me* to take over control of the Tower Law. Only I wrecked the Law, destroyed it. Or, I hope I did – I meant to.'

I paused to see if that got any comment. It didn't. I said, 'I ran away from the City. I left with a Hulta leader, a chieftan, I suppose you'd say. We were going to be married. That was the life I had, and what I'd chosen. What I *wanted*.'

I had to hesitate again, to stop my voice going shaky. He didn't interrupt. I said, 'On the morning of my marriage, before the wedding, I was grabbed by three City men, pushed in one of their hot-air balloons, taken to the coast and thrown on a ship. Two of them – Yazkool, Hrald – brought me here. I thought originally I was supposed to be taken to the City, but now I'm not even sure of that. Yazkool and Hrald put me in that house across the gulf. Then you sent Grembilard and he brought me here, to the Rise. Which I'd never heard of, and which I'd never have wanted to come to if I had.'

He just sat there.

I cried out at him, 'I've *lost* everything I wanted. Don't you understand? I was happy. How would I want to be made a prisoner and forced to come here, all these trees, miles from – away from –' I bit back the stream of words. But I'd clenched my fists, my hair felt standing-up and bristly as hedgehog quills.

81

The rain had ended. The high window was clearing to its pre-sunset spice shade.

'You expect me to believe this?' he said.

Yes, I did expect that. Why else had I made such a fuss. Trying to convince him.

'Very dramatic, Lady Claidis, if rather overdone. You're a good actress. They did warn me.'

I managed to speak level as a pavement.

'Who warned you?'

'I think you'd better see the letter. After all, it's about you.'

As he went over to a carved cupboard in the far wall, and opened its doors, (I couldn't see inside) the owl-bird undid one eye the colour of the sky. Then the eye and the doors closed, and he was offering me a sheet of paper.

Looking at this paper now, it's odd. It's not like any paper I ever saw before – not, for example, like the paper in this book on which I'm writing, with my ink pencil. Thinner yet stronger. Very white.

And the writing is printed, like in a book.

Is this the 'flying letter' someone mentioned earlier? I should have asked him.

What it said – I'll copy it down.

'TO PRINCE VENARION YLLAR KASLEM-IDOROS' (So that's how it goes.)

'WE TRUST YOU ARE IN GOOD HEALTH, AND PLEASANTLY OCCUPIED AMID YOUR LUXURIOUS JUNGLES.

'IT HAS BECOME NECESSARY THAT WE ASK YOUR ASSISTANCE. WE MUST ACCORDINGLY INSTRUCT YOU TO ACCEPT, INTO YOUR PALACE, A YOUNG WOMAN OF THE TOWERS. YOU WILL KNOW HER AS THE LADY CLAIDIS STAR.

'IT IS OUR SAD DUTY TO WARN YOU THAT SHE IS

AN IMMATURE AND EXCITABLE CREATURE, GIVEN TO RAGES, TANTRUMS AND, SHALL WE SAY, TO *INVENTING* QUITE CONVINCING STORIES OF HER OWN LIFE. (SHE MAY EVEN DENY HER OWN NAME.)

'WE ARE AWARE, THIS IS NOT THE MOST SUITABLE GUEST FOR YOU TO RECEIVE, WHEN, IN ANY CASE, YOU ARE MORE AT EASE WITH THE MECHANICALS AND TOYS OF YOUR PALACE. UNFORTUNATELY WE MUST INSIST. THIS CLAIDIS STAR HAS CAUSED QUARRELS AND UPSETS IN SEVERAL PLACES, WITHIN THE CITY AND OUTSIDE IT. HER DEMANDS TO VISIT THE RISE, WHICH SHE DECLARES NEEDFUL FOR HER EDUCATION, CAN NO LONGER BE IGNORED.

'OUR GRATITUDE TO YOU, PRINCE VENARION, WE HOPE WILL OFFSET, TO SOME EXTENT, THIS DISRUPTION TO YOUR PERSONAL ROUTINES.

'WE REMAIN, GREATLY IN YOUR DEBT: —'

I should have questioned him. Denied it. I don't know. There didn't seem any point. I certainly should have *demanded* (the letter says I do that, after all) to know *who* they were that sent it.

Because I saw the signature, and it's here, in front of me, but I was so destroyed by all of this, I just didn't —

I mean, after I read this, he showed me to the door, which gave on the steps down to the gardens. He said, polite, 'The rain's stopped.' And I just went out and he closed the door, and there I was with this paper, stumbling down the stairs (and trying not to cry and feeling ashamed because I think I did cry) — and *desperate*.

To say *I* lied, and to lie about *me* like that.

As if they knew me and I was one of them and they'd been so kind to me and I'd been an evil trouble-maker, and they'd *had* to send me here, where I insisted I wanted to go, before I did something even worse –

You see, I didn't know what to do. Don't.

So, I walked back across the gardens, and the sunset started and finished, then I got to the Rose Room somehow, even in its new place. The afterglow was dying on the walls, clashing nastily with all the curdled pinks in here.

The Star will come up soon.

These *lies* –

Oh what am I going to do?

To be in this mess and to be blamed for it and to be lied about –

The signature. I didn't say yet. Well, this was how their letter was signed. It was signed 'We'. That was all. *We*.

My Enemy

Perhaps I could write some of it up now. I haven't been able to touch this, not for a while.

(Even now, with this book propped on my knees, I feel . . . . . .)

After the Scene in his room, some more time passed, sliced into days and nights. I kept thinking now really was the time to go. After all, I'd seen, it was simple to get out. But the vrabburrs and other possible *things* put me off. Which wasn't brave, but perhaps sensible.

I started to think about a weapon, and wondered if there were any rifles or other guns in the Rise. But I can't fire a gun, and anyway don't like the idea of shooting at things, even things with nine-foot-long pointed teeth.

Also I thought I was at my wits' end. If only I'd known – !

One thing. I said to Jotto. 'I'm not comfortable in this

room. It may move again, and all this pink is making me feel queasy.'

'It *is* a bit ukky,' agreed Jotto.

He was definitely more concerned about the colour scheme than the moving-around stuff, and actually got down to it, and by that afternoon I'd been put into a kind of pavilion on the lawns, which is all pillars, and rather good tiles in the bathroom, and *always*, they say, stays still.

Treacle came at once and watered some pots of flowers on the steps (in the usual manner.)

'I wish you could talk,' I'd tactlessly lamented.

She just did her wriggle-giggle, didn't care.

That evening, which was four days after the Scene, Jotto brought me some supper.

'You're forgetting to eat. You're still in a mood, aren't you, dear?'

'You bet I am.'

'Tsk,' tsked Jotto. 'And him all funny and off his food too. Like my chickens, frankly, both of you. It really is the end. It's so difficult, *getting* any food, and then making it look appealing. I mean, I could just slop it all down in a heap, but no, I *arrange* it in patterns, and put orchids (please note the orchid, dear) by the plates, and choose glasses that *match* – and what do I get? Does anyone swoon with joy? No. *You* nibble or gobble or sulk and won't eat it, and then the wild-life gets it. And now *he's* prowling round and round up there in his tower, and that owl ate his lunch – I *know*, I *saw* some nut-butter on its feathers – and it's not supposed to *do* that – Oh, it's too much.'

'What a shame your prince isn't eating,' I said sweetly, 'if he ate something he might choke on it.'

'There you are, you see. This unfriendly *atmosphere*.'

I thought, Venn's decidedly not upset about me, so what's got to him now? Or is he just in a state because he had to *talk* to me for five minutes?

Nothing happened that day, I just wandered about, climbing up small hills and peering into pools with golden fish in them. (Hrald would probably have run to get a fishing-net.)

The gardens are beautiful, it's true. Like the House Garden, but better, more genuinely wild, more interestingly cultivated. I saw the Gardener once. He was shouting at some monkeys in the trees. Maybe wishing them fleas or something.

At dusk I saw a great trail of bats go over from the real cliffy parts below. Then, on the twilight, the white owl sailed across, just before the Star came up and blotted everything with its too-harsh light.

I never thought I'd say a star was horrible.

But the Wolf Star is.

It's revolting. Too bright, too large, too *there*.

I've never seen it come up from the eastern horizon, always missed that. It's always suddenly just looming up over the gardens, slowly going on across the sky and away behind the Rise, and then gradually slinking back – it seems to set in the east, where it rises – just as too-big and too-bright, in the last night hours. In the pavilion, whose windows are clear and only veiled with muslin, it woke me every night.

If the moon is up when the Star comes, the moon looks like a poor blue ghost beside it.

However. After the owl soared off over the trees, I went in. I had another bath and went to bed, because I couldn't think of anything at all to do. I didn't write in this book, hadn't written anything after the last bit. The bit that ended '*We*'.

During the night the Star didn't wake me, coming back, for once. Instead I dreamed the owl flew in at a window I'd left open. It flew round the room and I thought, I'm dreaming about the owl flying round the room, and that was all.

In the morning I did notice a window I'd thought I'd shut was open. Then Jotto arrived and I went out and had breakfast with them, Grem and Treacle and some cats, under the huge flowering tree.

When I came *back*, I pulled the bag out from under the pavilion bed. I wanted something I'd left in it. I don't remember what it was, because I never found it. Which was because I didn't look for it. And that was because, in the bag, what I didn't also find, and that at once, was *this*. I mean this book.

I mean, it was gone.

Naturally I turned the pavilion's three rooms upside down. Even the bath-chamber and the little side room full of old gardening things and a statue of a large porcupine.

I hadn't brought much with me and most of that I'd left in the bag. I had this sense always now of just making camp, whatever room or apartment I was in.

When I'd looked everywhere, including pulling the bed-clothes off and dragging the mattress on to the floor, I looked everywhere again.

Then I ran to the doorway and began screaming for Jotto and next for Grembilard.

Some monkeys answered from a tall tamarind.

After that I recalled a bell-pull thing in the pavilion,

rushed back and yanked on it so hard it broke and fell down.

I thought no one would come. (They'd all gone off after breakfast.) I started running about up and down outside the pavilion.

Now and then I've read of people 'tearing their hair' – and I was. I was, as they say, beside myself. What I felt was worse than anything – even fear, though it was a sort of fear. Indescribable, or I could cover pages. Panic, loss, fright. And *shame*. Why shame? Of course, you'll see at once, although I didn't.

Then abruptly there was Grembilard, and Jotto too.

'Is something wrong?' asked Grembilard.

I shrieked 'My book – my book's disappeared!'

'Oh my,' said Jotto. Then, sensibly, 'Don't fret, lady, we'll find it. What was the cover like, and what was the title?'

'Oh you – oh – it wasn't that sort of – it was –' I floundered. In my head I heard Nemian that time/s on our journey to the Wolf Tower, patronizingly calling it my 'Diary'. 'Diary!' I screamed, hopping from foot to foot. 'My diary.'

'Oh, um,' said Jotto.

Grembilard said, 'It can't have gone far, madam.'

'I've looked – everywhere – everywhere –' I scrambled after them back into the pavilion. I stood cursing them as they wasted time looking carefully everywhere I had, (including under the mattress and behind the stone porcupine.) At the same moment I was praying that they somehow *would* find the book where it couldn't be.

They didn't.

'Could you have left it under the tree at breakfast?'

I knew I hadn't, but I bolted for the tree. I rummaged round its roots amid fallen toast and flowers.

The monkeys yelled with laughter.

I *wouldn't* cry again.

'Well, lady, it looks as if it isn't here.'

'Oh – *Jotto* – !!!'

'Perhaps, while you were walking, madam –'

Trying to be calm. 'No, I did take the bag, but I didn't take the book out. I know I didn't –'

I wavered. Wondering now if I had. I hadn't trusted the pavilion to keep still, not really. If I was going to be more than a few strides away – I lugged that bag with me, and on every long walk. Tired, I'd sling it down and sit on it. I *never* took out this book – I hadn't wanted to, afraid of reading bits over and feeling worse.

But if I had, and had forgotten – maybe left it somewhere for a monkey to play with, *eat* –

All the things that have happened to me, and I'd kept hold of it. This book, which somehow meant and means so much, because I have filled it with my own truths, and almost everything that I've seen and felt. In this book I wrote how I first met Argul. I wrote about that first time he kissed me.

I will NOT cry.

Some monkey has it up a tree. That's why they're making that terrible row. They've eaten my book, my *life* – and it's given them indigestion –

Or a bird's found it and flown –

I went completely still.

'Oops,' said Jotto. 'She's going to have a turn.'

'The window,' I said, staring at him coldly. 'My dream. The *owl* –'

It was Jotto's mouth that dropped open. Why is he so human? Grem, the human one, stood there like a machine.

Jotto asked, 'She means the prince's owl?'

'Yes I do. It was in my room. I thought I dreamed it. The owl took my book!'

I spun round and began to run again. The grass whirled by under my feet. I leapt over flower-beds and through clawing bamboos. *They* cantered after me.

I was plainly heading for the rock-tower. His place.

'Don't,' I grunted 'try to stop me –'

'But – but –' called Jotto, not out of breath, because he doesn't have to breathe, but still somehow breathless, 'he's not there!'

I faltered, not meaning to, tripped on something and flopped over.

Grem and Jotto helped me out of the oleanders.

'Prince Venn isn't in his room,' said Grem. He shook his head to underline that.

'How – *convenient* – as if – I'd believe you.'

'Look for yourself,' said Jotto. 'I carried his breakfast up all those stairs – and there he was, gone.'

'I'll see for myself.'

They let me, only escorting me. His door doesn't open unless it 'recognizes' you. Like the door in the Wolf Tower. Jotto explained this.

In the eight-sided room, the thieving owl dozed on its perch. Red silk veils dimmed the windows. All those books. Were any of them mine? No, this book doesn't look like that. I wanted to search anyway, pull all the books down and open every cupboard and drawer. They wouldn't let me. I gave up struggling. Both of them are strong.

'Where does he go then, your charming prince who steals things – gets his pet *owl* to steal them – things that belong to other people – where does he go when he isn't here?'

'He might be anywhere, lady,' said Jotto, looking quite

unhappy. 'And if he's in the palace – well, with it always moving –'

I wanted to scream and scream. To behave the way the evil letter had said I did – and perhaps I do. Do I? But I walked out and down the steps. I didn't want to stay in his room. And the owl, though I could have wrung its feathery neck (well, I couldn't; it was an owl) had only done what he'd somehow made it do.

Why?

Why . . .

Was he even now curled up somewhere, a cooling drink to hand, reading my book?

Reading my truths, my life? About the House and the Law and Argul's kiss?

I threw myself on the ground. I behaved as they said, as I'd seen my foul mistress at the House, Jade Leaf, behave. A Tantrum.

'Oh dear, you've quite flattened this fern.'

'*Go away.*'

'Poor lady. I'm sure he didn't mean to upset –'

I drowned him with my shouts.

But in the end I stood up. I shook myself, dragged my hands over my cheeks to dry them.

'Is she better or worse?' whispered Jotto.

'Worse, I think.' Grem.

Treacle had crept up. She half hid herself behind a tree. I'd never seen her look so serious.

I said, quietly, 'I shall look for him. I shall find him if it takes ten years. I shall kill him.'

Writing that now, it seems absurd. In a way that puzzles me too. My feeling was real, and justified – in a way. What Venn

91

had done – it was like reading my mind – my *heart* –

Worse than anything, my sheer *embarrassment*.

You see, he wasn't – isn't – you.

You, whoever You are, are far away from me, further away than the moon. And yet – nearer than anyone. Nearer even, perhaps, than Argul. If you've read my mind in these pages, I *invited* you into my head. And you, you had the kindness to accept and enter, and to be with me, through all of this.

Of course, I only made you up when I was alone. But no, I don't believe that. I believe you *are* there. Or you will be.

You're my guest, my friend.

Venn burgled me.

After my outburst, I sat down and said nothing else. I wouldn't answer either Grem or Jotto. Jotto went off and came back with some iced wine. I said, 'Thanks.' Didn't drink it.

They drew away. Well, they'd all been warned. I was 'excitable' and 'immature', given to rages, a liar.

I suppose it was the last straw. How many last straws does it take.

As I remember, I meant to rest, and then get up and start my search. I madly thought the calmer I looked, the easier it would be to get away from G and J, and maybe T, when the right time came.

I had no fears now of the moveable palace, of vrabburrs, or of anything.

But the day, like the rooms, moved on and around.

The shadows had got longer, and an afternoon heat-stillness powdered the trees.

Then one of those yellow birds began to go *clink-clink*. I looked up, and Venn was standing there, just across from me.

If I'd had any doubts, I needn't have. He was holding this book in his hand.

(In fact his name, properly spelled, is Ven'n – being short for Venarion with the *ario* left out.)

I got up slowly.

Grem and Jotto must have been there. I don't think I saw them, can't remember them. Really there was nothing, just a shadow-sunny static void, with Ven'n-Venn drawn like a dark line through its middle.

He was looking at me. I mean properly.

He was seeing me.

He said, 'Grem says you've vowed to kill me.'

'That's right.'

'Suppose I didn't read it?'

'Why take it then?'

'Well, perhaps I *meant* to read it – and couldn't. Your handwriting's pretty awful, Claidi.'

I started at him. I don't know what I would really have done, and no doubt Grem would have stopped me anyway. Even Venn might have been able to. But in the rush of fire that was throwing me forward, I heard it again. My name. Not Claidissa or Claidis. *Claidi.*

So I swerved. I grabbed hold of a tree and swung against its trunk, and he said, 'You have worse enemies than me, Claidi. Look.'

And then he did something to this book, something to its back, and a little bright object, like a tiny flat button, dropped out from inside it, and he caught it in his free hand.

'What's that?' I stupidly asked. Claidi, always asking questions.

'That,' he said, 'is how the Wolf Tower tracked you and

found you. By that private pool on your wedding day, where the balloon came down. *This* was in your book all the time. They could come and get you whenever they wanted.'

'They – my book.'

This book. They had found me because of something (scientific – magical) put into this book. He couldn't really tell me how it worked, that is, when he did try to tell me. He said, Imagine a light shining miles away and you just go towards that light – and the thing in the book was like that, only it wasn't a light. If it had been a light, *I'd* have seen it.

But because of it, they'd found me. Taken me, brought me *here*. This book too had been – my enemy?

IN THE DARK

'What are you looking at?'

'I'm watching weather coming. Those clouds. The way you can see storms start long before they get here.'

'Looking for the future eh, Claidi? Perhaps you're looking the wrong way.'

We just had that exchange, on this high wide balcony facing east. Venn and I. (We've been trapped here two days.)

He says clever things like that.

But he doesn't really talk to you, though. To one. I mean, he doesn't meet your eyes, when he speaks or as you do, or only for a moment, one huge gaze, and then away. Is it his disgust, of is he – afraid?

He hasn't known many people, apparently.

Says he prefers *reading* about people, even being *told* about people, to being with them.

He said, for example: 'It's always preferable to read

94

about a place, rather than to go there. And reading about something, anything, is better than living the experience. One has distance, and there's time to examine the events. And if one needs to go over them again, there they are, the same, in black and white.'

He then added, 'After all, isn't that why you write everything down in your book?'

I replied bitterly, 'Oh, I'm sharp as a spoon.'

He'd blinked.

It's a Hulta expression, actually it goes 'Hu–yath mai rar, ai: She/he's sharp as a spoon, she/he is. It seems funny, but Blurn once told me that, in older times, the Hulta used to sharpen the stems of their spoons, in case they ever needed them as weapons, so it's not as daft as it sounds.

I told Venn this.

He said, 'You see, that's very interesting.'

We had *this* conversation, if such it was, some days ago, in various parts of the gardens.

Before we got to that, though, we'd stood there in the afternoon, him still holding this book. And then he called Grem, who appeared. 'Give her this back, will you.'

Grem brought me the book. I was able to take it from Grem. But then I just dropped it on the ground. It wasn't mine any more.

Then Venn said, 'Shall we sit down?' as if we were in a sitting-room. And he sat on the ground, and then I sat on the ground too, where I'd been before, with my back against a tree. Grem and Jotto – and Treacle – had vanished again.

He and I were about fifteen feet apart.

I'd needed to sit. Now I just stared at him, and of course he didn't even try to meet my eyes.

'I know how you must feel, Claidi.'

'Do you? I doubt it.'

'To take that, to read that – yes, unforgiveable.' I didn't say anything, (I didn't want to talk to him at all. At the same moment I wanted to shout at him on and on.) 'You see, Grem mentioned you were writing something.'

'*Did* he.'

'I hadn't questioned him about you, Claidi. At that point I didn't want to know anything about you. I confess, that's why I half wanted you left in the outer rooms. Perhaps later I might have been interested to hear about what you did at the House, and in the Tower. But then, I wasn't sure what you'd tell me would be true.'

I bit my tongue not to start shouting about the Letter.

Venn said, 'Grem simply told me you kept busy and didn't cause any trouble. You walked a lot, and you wrote in a book. I realized it was a kind of diary.'

'It isn't.'

'No,' he said, 'it's more a journal.'

I refused to like this much-better sounding description.

Venn said, 'Then, after we spoke last –'

'Is *that* what you'd call it?'

'I felt uneasy. Well, Claidi. I don't know people very much. There's Treacle, and Grem, of course, and there was dear old Heepo, before we lost him –'

(??)

'And my mother, I suppose, if I can count her. She was very stern and distant. She went away when I was nine . . . Anyway, how could I judge you? You seemed genuine. But I was in the dark.'

I sizzled. Tried not to.

He gave me one of those quick wide glances, and said, 'I thought, if you kept a journal, you might have put down the truth in it. Of course, I could be wrong there, too. Maybe your journal is all lies and dreams and mad made-up nonsense –'

I yelled then. I yelled quite a lot.

He looked alarmed, and then he just sat there, looking at the broken-off fern frond he was turning in his fingers.

What did I say (yell)? Can't remember. (He's right. I should have written it down and *then* yelled it.) Somehow I'd forgotten about the sinister button thing in the binding. What I said was all about truth, and my being truthful, about that Letter, what he'd done, and I must have gone on for a while.

In the end I just hadn't the energy to continue. There was a long silence.

'God, Claidi. Yes, I'm sorry. Sorry. I should throw myself off the Rise.'

'*Why don't you then?*'

'Because I'm a coward,' he said. Just that. And then I saw – well, he was crying. I mean, it was almost like Treacle. Tears just ran down his face. And then stopped. But unlike Treacle he had for a few seconds that cold-in-the-head sound one has, if one cries.

In this voice he said, 'Please understand, I don't expect you to forgive me. This isn't an excuse, only an explanation. I just didn't know any better. I don't know how I should behave to another person. Not really. I've never had much chance to find out.' By then his voice had cleared. He said, crisply, 'They'd told me you were – well you read their letter. But I started to have doubts. I thought your book would prove it one way or the other. It has. *They* lied. *Not* you. And you – are *you*. And because you are, I am *ashamed*.'

I got up and walked off. Somehow I'd picked this book up, too, and I took it with me.

He let me go. No one followed. I ended up quite lost in the gardens, in a jungly bit (like 'dear old Heepo'?)

I raged, naturally. How could he act so wickedly and then *cry* – but I kept thinking, it was just what a very young child might do. A kid who did something bad because – it didn't know any better. And then it saw the damage and got upset. I mean, he wasn't crying for himself. What had *he* got to lose? He was crying . . . because he'd done this to me.

But then I thought, Maybe he thinks everyone has to love him and think he's nice and wonderful, and he cries when he does something unspeakable so we'll say, Oh poor Venn, look how sad he is. Better forgive him, he didn't mean it.

Sunset arrived.

It was when the awful Star rose I remembered the bright awful thing which had fallen out of the binding of this book.

I decided I'd go and find him after all and demand what that was all about.

But next I ridiculously couldn't find a way out of the jungle area, especially in the dark as the Star moved on.

Finally I heard Jotto calling in a timid voice. I let him find me.

Jotto said, 'Er, lady dear, there's some lovely supper but he did say – um – would you sit and eat with him – outdoors?'

'Oh all right,' I graciously barked.

Supper was under the flowering tree near my pavilion. (The flowers give off a marvellous perfume at night.) Several cats and other things soon arrived. They always do. (Jotto says a monkey can hear a pie or a mango being sliced from half a mile away.)

Deeply dark black sky and the stars and moon looking washed and shiny, since the Star had moved on. (It seemed to go faster that night.)

I won't put down all the conversation. I couldn't follow all of it anyway, the things he 'explained'.

And I still don't know what I think of him.

He looked all right. He had on this white shirt with fringes on the cuffs.

Oh anyway.

I will make a note of the supper – it was – well, under other circumstances I'd have been fascinated, delighted. Not so much by the food, though that was delicious (it usually is, here.) How it was served.

I thought Jotto was going to serve it, as he normally does if he's around. But he sat down by Grem. Treacle was there too, with her spiky black hair brushed up spikier, and long gold earrings. (I was the only scruff-bag, in my now tatty dress from the Rose Room.)

Tall candles burned in globes of pale amber. By this light, up a strange little ramp I'd been wondering about, the first dish was drawn on to the table.

It was a big silver dish, with a fresh salad arranged like jewels by Jotto. But the dish was attached by a harness arrangement to a team of tiny black and white rabbits! I do mean tiny. They were each the size of a *mouse*. There were ten of them in all. They galloped forward and pulled up to a perfect finish. Then just stood there until a beaming Jotto, (saying 'Aren't they *sweet*?') unharnessed them.

Then other dishes came in procession. Five blue hippos, about the size of kittens, brought vegetables. Ten black-necked geese, the size of sparrows, brought a train of hot sauces. Two very strong little tigapards, each as big as a blackbird, hauled up a large pie on a gold tray. Three fat mouse-size mice – that also looked like *pigs* (they had curly tails, and snouts – *pouces*?) brought a china castle of assorted nut-cheeses.

They all managed faultlessly, except for the tigapards, which, as soon as they saw us all, promptly sat down, and had to be helped lug the pie, by Treacle.

Once released, all these creatures ambled about the table, playing with each other, and accepting pieces of food, but only when offered to them. Well, one of the pouces (pice?) did drag a banana away behind the salt cellar, but never mind.

They really were lovely, these little animals.

When I asked, they told me, Venn told me mostly, that they're not dolls, are quite real. They'd been bred, like the vrabburrs. 'Not everything she did,' said Venn, meaning his mother, 'was dangerous.'

'Where do they live?'

'They have a big hutch and enclosure in the gardens,' said Jotto. Grem added, 'They're taken in at night.'

The supper was relaxed. It was hard to be nervy and angry, with mouse-size rabbits playing kick-ball with a radish, and a miniature tigapard purring in your lap.

I did think, *This is clever. I shouldn't fall for this*.

But I fell for it.

The wine was pink, in rose-amber glasses.

I heard myself laugh at something Jotto said. And then he, Venn, laughed. As if I'd said he was now allowed to.

I've wondered about him and Treacle. He's grown up with her, seems fond of her. But she's a wild thing, Treacle. She's called that, they say, because she always liked treacle.

He doesn't treat any of them like slaves. That says something about him. Maybe?

They all *know* each other. They know Jotto, though he was, obviously, always an 'adult', even when they were kids.

What was that like, growing up in this bizarre place?

He says his mother was close to him only when he was very small, and he remembers being two years old, because he has a clear picture of walking in the gardens with her, and she said to him, 'You're two, now, Venarion.' And after that, she changed.

'She didn't touch me any more,' he said, 'she used to hug me before that,' drinking the wine, seeming so casual, so I knew he wasn't, it still distresses him. 'She became cold and uncaring. I seldom saw her. Before, she used to read me stories. Once she changed, I had to read them myself. Grem would help me hold the books, they were so heavy.'

He could read at two years old!!

'I bored her,' said Venn, laughing again. 'Well, she was a very clever woman. A scientist — what your Hulta would call a magician. She did all this. Made the rooms move, bred the animals — the cats with the plated skulls, the vrabburrs, these little ones on the table. She made other experiments. Grem's hair, for example. And Treacle's tears.' (I wondered if they minded, but they didn't look bothered.)

Jotto even said, 'Don't forget *me*.'

'Yes, of course, Jotto, the most brilliant of all mechanical dolls. The other three, across the ravines — they weren't so good. But Jotto's magnificent, aren't you, Jott?'

'I am,' said Jotto, 'though I say it myself.'

'In a way,' said Venn, cheerful, smiling at the moon, 'I'd say I was her experiment, too. After all, she made me, didn't she, even though I'm only flesh and blood. Her son. So I think I was the least successful experiment of them all. The only one that didn't work as it — I — was supposed to. Then

101

anyway she got tired of all of us.'

He'd gently lifted up a pouce, and I thought he was going to dunk it in the sauce by mistake. But he realized in time and put it carefully back on the table.

After that, they changed the subject, all four of them, the way a family can do things like that, acting as one.

We played clever word games. Grem sang a very funny song about earwigs, and Jotto produced a flute and started the nightingales singing. (Some of the nightingales are clockwork too. Put there to 'encourage' the others.)

Later, Treacle and Jotto were running races. They were always neck and neck. And Grem strolled off to talk to the Gardener, who suddenly appeared like a grumpy phantom, across the lawn.

Venn looked at me, slightly longer than usual. So *I* looked away.

He said softly, 'You know, I really couldn't read a lot of it, Claidi. Your handwriting – is a little like another language.'

I frowned. 'Just tell me about the *thing* in the book.'

'It's a Tag. You've been patient, waiting so long to ask me.'

I'd forgotten actually. Incredible, but a fact.

However, now he said he'd answer whatever he could, including the questions I posed in my 'journal'.

And when he said that, for a second everything seemed much easier, *because* he'd read this book. How strange. How awful. But it did.

THE QUEST FOR THE LIBRARY

Her name is (was) Ustareth. His mother.

That was question number – let me look back and see –

102

No. 4) or part of it. As to who she was, no one *I'd* know, it goes without saying.

I think I'll answer these questions here, in the order I put them before. (He would approve of that, writing it down and then writing it out again with the solutions, in the right order. I'm not doing it because he would approve.)

Here goes.

1) Why am I here? *Not* because I asked to come here. He doesn't know. He said this: 'They sent you here to worry me, I think. I don't – didn't want visitors. But mostly they did it to punish you. You messed them about. So they've messed *you* about.'

2) When can I leave? No, he didn't answer that. I didn't *ask* it, in fairness. Because now there seems so much to sort out here, perhaps I have to stay a while.

3) Why did V's mother – Ustareth – make the rooms move? Her experiment. To see if she could. To have fun. To stop herself being bored.

4) Who was she – answered. Or as much as I can, so far.

5) Why did she go and *where*? He'd said because she was fed up with it all. Into the jungle, so presumably *through* the jungle and off somewhere else? But he looked very odd over this one, which is reasonable. Didn't press it.

6) and 7) The hard light in the lamps – Yes, the waterfall creates the power for this, as it does for some of the clockwork, and for certain other things ... we didn't somehow quite sort out if this included the food. But it turns out Jotto doesn't always cook, he simply has to go and collect it – ? Then he arranges it and brings it. I'll have to go through this one again, I didn't follow it really. Oh, and the waterfall power thing is something about hydro–something.

No, I didn't understand that at all, though Venn went over it two or three times. It works though.

8) Talking to Venn. I am.

9) That question about the furballs. (V says what the Gardener shouts at the monkeys means 'May your fur turn to iron'.) (Fine.)

We talked a very long time before I went off exhaustedly to sleep.

The worrying thing is, because he read this book, or some of it (most of it I suspect) he partly knows me.

But I don't know him.

And yet – I almost feel I *do* – also because he read this. And that I can't explain to myself.

As if in exchange, he did say a lot about his childhood. In clever, off-hand sentences. It sounded, underneath, miserable, but also – glorious. All that freedom. But, the not having a mother.

He knows I didn't ever know my parents.

He said, 'We have to go to the Rise library. There's information there, things about the Tower Families, the history of the Towers, and so on. It might help you. The trouble is, of course, *finding* the library. It, naturally, moves too. And quite randomly. It'll be murder.'

'Tell me about the flying letter.'

'I don't think I can. I mean you won't understand.'

'Try.'

'Claidi, I mean *I* don't understand. I never have. And I've only ever got three. Four, counting the lying one about you. They just – appear – out of the wall.'

'Oh.'

So the flying letter and the thing, which Venn calls a Tag, and which they put in this book, remain a mystery.

Who put the Tag into the binding though?

Probably Ironel Novendot. But I suppose even Nemian could have done it. To make sure I didn't stray. Perhaps when he saw I was getting interested in someone else, in Argul. Perhaps Nemian slipped the Tag in under the binding as we travelled. The book wasn't always with me, but in a wagon.

It left no mark I could see. But then the book was already a bit travel-worn. And how would I ever think such a thing was possible and so look out for it?

'I've seen such things before,' Venn said. 'So I checked. It didn't surprise me, to find it.'

The House had candles and oil lamps. And Peshamba had crystals that watched you, and dolls – but not like Jotto. The City on the River had nothing much . . . just watchers, lift-lifters worked by slaves, and balloons. And the doors could recognize you. And they had the Law.

'They all have the Law,' said Venn. 'In some form. The House had all those rituals you disliked so much. And there are other places, with other rules.'

I said, 'What about here?'

'No, there's nothing like that here. Perhaps my – when she came here, Ustareth, she hoped to escape the Law and the rituals.'

Something nags at me. If you dare read this again, Ven'n, though I don't think you will (I hope you won't) then here it is. The Rise does have its own version of the stupid and mindless Law-type rituals and rules, designed to get in the way and make life difficult and chancy. It's the *rooms moving about*. Isn't it?

We prepared for the trek solemnly and with care. As if for a great expedition into unknown lands.

Jotto and Grem were to carry a lot of things, including water-bottles — there are bathrooms everywhere, but you can't always be sure the water is drinkable.

Treacle also carries some stuff, and I volunteered too, but they didn't give me much.

I'd packed the pink dress with my WD, and wore this grey-white one I brought from the house over the gulf. (And, I packed this book, although I hadn't written in it and thought I might not, again. But, as you've seen, that didn't last.)

Venn also carried things in a bag on his back.

The funniest thing was the team of six cats Jotto and Grem rounded up and harnessed to a sort of sled, to carry light bedding and other bits and pieces.

Venn drew a rough map before we started.

'The library is often *here*.' He pointed at the spot he'd marked in a tangle of squares and circles and snake-like coilings that were apparently rooms, corridors, courtyards.

Jotto particularly looked glum.

'Only doubtless it won't be there,' Venn went on. 'It had a phase,' he added, 'of travelling east then south, then back north and west. So we could try for that, to start with.'

'But what about the time it just kept going up and up?' said Jotto. 'It was on the sixth gallery once, rumbling about between those towers —'

I stopped listening really. It sounded hopeless, frankly. Why were we doing it? For me, it seems . . .

We left the gardens about mid-morning.

The cliff-palace loomed over us, swallowed us up in its caves of painted stone.

For about an hour we walked steadily, and although we heard *sounds* of parts of the Rise moving, everything round us stayed still, as it was once supposed to when someone was there.

'Though just walking about in a room can set it off now,' said Jotto. 'I should know. The times I've been trapped for *days*.'

Once or twice peculiar mechanical things appeared and went rattling past. That is, they went *past* because we all quickly got out of their way – they seemed likely to knock you flying otherwise, and some were as large as a sheep. They are cleaners, Jotto said, sniffily. Once too there was a sort of spider thing, crawling over a ceiling, touching up the paint-work.

Soon however, we were just going out through a wide arch, when an enormous staircase came pouring out of a wall. It rolled right at us (reminding me of the storm-waves on the ship) and stopped with a thud only when it had blocked the arch. Meanwhile we'd scattered yelling, and the cats had overturned the sled.

Jotto and Treacle and I gathered up sheets and Grem mended the broken harness.

'We'll have to go *that* way instead,' said Venn, waving the map.

This became the chorus to our crazy journey. Oh, this way's now impassable. We'll go *that* way then.

But *that* way was often found to be blocked too, or had gone off itself somewhere else.

Four days went by. And *four* nights. Unbelievable, I know, but worse was to come.

Books at the House were sometimes adventures. Some of them had titles like *Hunting the Treasure Hoard* or *Quest for the Emerald Queen*.

Well, this must be the *Quest for the Library*.

In a sane book, one would travel over plains, across mountains, through deep woods. Here we slog on and on through this ghastly palace. In the book, probably we'd be getting somewhere. Here, we're always miles away. I do mean miles.

On the *fifth* day we got stuck. In here.

We'd got caught before, once, on day three, when an apartment we were crossing abruptly took off – so fast Treacle and Jotto and I fell over!

The apartment, which was of several rooms with inner curtained doorways – if there are no closing wood doors, the whole thing tends to move together, Venn said – rushed around for nearly an hour and then stopped dead in an area dark enough the hard light came on.

When we looked, there was no way out, the three outer doors were covered by walls now directly outside. Luckily after only ten minutes the apartment went off again. Soon as we could we all charged out into a stone courtyard with a statue (of a huge rat or something). We only just made it, too, before the apartment swung away again. (We walked past this same apartment the day before yesterday, I think. It looked the same. Fortunately we didn't need to go through.)

Anyway, the evening of the day before yesterday, we made camp at dinnertime facing the foot of a vast staircase. We left quite a gap between us and it, of course, in case it suddenly moved. It didn't move though. Jotto set up the brazier and Grem lit it, for tea.

It's extremely weird. Unless there are the lights, which often there haven't been, sitting round this kind of brazier-campfire, late at night, in the middle of a *building*. Shadows gather blackly at the edges of the light, just as they do outdoors. Even eyes sometimes gleam there, watching cats or other things (?) that Venn says live in the palace.

In the morning we were woken about dawn by the rooms behind us thundering off like a herd of rhino.

Venn consulted his map and said we ought to climb the staircase. This obviously was tricky, especially for five of us and six cats pulling a sled.

He said we'd do it this way: me and Jotto together, then him, Treacle and Grem (carrying the cats and the sled.) This way, even if separated, no one should be stranded totally alone.

I was jittery, climbing that stair, I can tell you. But we all made it – almost.

Treacle, clutching three cats, was on the last landing, when the *lower* stair split away. It was a fearful sight. She seemed to be hanging in space, but then her piece of stair just rose gracefully upwards. As it sailed past us, she was able to jump off into Grem's arms. One of the cats bit him in the excitement.

Leaving the stair-top soaring on up into a dome, we came out into this massive hall with cream-yellow walls, a gallery, and a gigantic window and balcony facing east.

There were books in stacks built into the walls.

'Is this the library?'

'No,' said Venn. 'It's the Little Book Room.'

'I see.' It was about a hundred yards long and about the same wide.

We had a late breakfast in here. (Jotto kept muttering about his chickens, which he had left the Gardener to feed.) Then we had a look at some of the books, (most of which seemed to be written in different languages.)

I climbed up an inner stair to the gallery, and went out on to the balcony. I was admiring the view over the gardens, the descending jungle-cliff beyond – when the Little Book

Room began slowly moving its Little self. It was so gentle, it really didn't seem much to worry about. From the balcony, it was quite fun.

The LBR glided along and along the third storey. Trees went by below, some with monkeys staring up curiously. I even glimpsed the Gardener, bending in an annoyed way over a lotus pond. *Then* the LBR began to *rise*. This too was smooth enough, but we went up and up – Where we settled, I'd say the ground was – well, a very long way down.

Behind us, the only exit has been closed off by another wall.

At first we all waited for the room to move again, but it hasn't.

Two days later, we're still here.

It wasn't a storm I saw gathering, from the balcony, just bubbly clouds. It's getting on for sunset now again. Jotto is stoking the brazier. Four of the cats are having a pretend-fight.

There are two bathrooms off this room. I had a bath in a yellow marble tub and washed my hair. For something to do. And to avoid Venn.

It's all right when we're travelling, or eating or something, but when he seeks me out, as he did on the balcony . . . It makes me uncomfortable. And his clever remarks – '*Looking for the future*'. He also said there are ghost mice in the library which eat the pages, and which have 'Eaten more than we can ever know.'

I wrote a lot of the last section locked in the bathroom while my hair dried.

There's a bedroom too, very small. Lemon-curd silk and white wood furniture. He avoided it and Jotto whispered to me, '*She* used to sleep there a lot, at times.'

She – Ustareth. Venn's mum.

I was nosy. I tried to open the cupboard doors and drawers, but none of them would. I thought – was I being as bad, doing that, as he was, reading my jour– my book?

He's made me feel I need to know things. This whole trek is supposed to be so I can learn more about the Towers. The Wolf Tower – the Law, the rituals, what *They* (?) are up to. But honestly, I don't want to know. Not really. But he's made me feel now I *have* to – or somehow I haven't got a chance.

How has he done that?

I am so aware of him all the time.

This huge room is too small for both of us to be in at once.

'The food's going to run out,' says Jotto, looking peeved. 'And I packed such *masses*. Look at this bread! And these pomegranates are all runny and squidgy.'

This is stupid. We're trapped miles from anywhere in a *room* in a *building* and we're going to *starve*.

Venn said, as if he didn't care much, 'She knew ways of making the rooms shift, if this happened.'

'Who? Your mother?' I asked, furious. 'Didn't she ever tell *you*?'

'She never told me anything, after I was two.'

'And you never tried to *learn* anything after you were two,' I nastily said.

Jotto looked upset and I wished I hadn't.

But Treacle turned a cartwheel, revealing she was wearing red and gold striped knickers. Which made us all laugh, for some reason.

After lunch or tea, whatever it was, I walked off to Her Room, again.

I did something awful. Maybe it wasn't. She's long gone, and if she'd cared about any of it, wouldn't she have taken it with her? Using a knife and fork from the meal, I started breaking into the drawers.

She could have fastened them by some *scientific* means, anyway. And she hadn't. No, I got them all open after about half an hour. It made a mess, chips and splinters and curly gilded locks all over the floor. (No one came to see what I was doing, though I hadn't been quiet.)

There was some jewellery. Very beautiful. Long tear-drop pearls, and a necklace of transparent polished green stones. A topaz in a ring.

When I saw the ring, I thought of what Grem had asked, about *my* ring, if it was my mother's, because it had 'properties'. Venn knows now it hasn't – because of course my ring came from the Hulta. But has this topaz got them? I picked it up cautiously. I even put it on my middle finger – it was quite a bit too big.

Then – I stole it. I do steal things. I stole this book. In the House, you only ever got anything by stealing.

But I felt guilty, even though I know I took the ring in case it's going to have some magical-scientific use.

It's in my bag, tied up in a cloth from the bathroom. So if you read this, Venn – you'd better not – then you'll know.

Apart from the jewellery I didn't find much. Most of the drawers and little cupboards were empty, just dust and sweet-smelling powders in the corners, and in one a little black key and a scrap of paper with nothing on it.

There was a closet that had only one door, and the door

had a bird painted on it. I didn't need to break in – the little key fitted it. The door opened. And there was this dress. Ivory satin, is how I'd guess it should be described, thickly sewn with pearls.

I pushed it aside and in the back of the closet was a lever with an enamel handle.

They used to say I had moods.

I'm in one.

I reached in and tried the lever, and when it moved I made it go over as far as it would. When I did, there was a really frightening noise – like hundreds of bricks crashing away into a bottomless pit. Perhaps that's what it was, because the back of the closet was now open, and beyond was another stair, narrow and dark and completely uninviting. It went down and down.

Although no one came to see before, this noise was so extreme, they all had, now.

They all stood there, gaping. But Venn wasn't gaping, he looked paper white. He said, 'I remember that dress.'

I said, 'Do you remember these *steps*? Are they safe? Do they go anywhere?'

'Yes . . . I think that's how she used to leave this room, or come up here, sometimes. I seem to recall that, how she'd just disappear, I couldn't find her . . .'

He turned as if to go off, but Grem caught his arm. Then they walked off together, and Grembilard had his arm round Venn. And I felt as if my stomach had turned to boiling soup and I could have slapped both of them. And me, for being so unkind.

Anyway, they've decided now, about – it seems – six months

later, we'll all use these stairs behind the closet to get out of here. They 'think' the closet stairs don't move. Let's hope they don't.

They did. *Did*! We're all separated – I'm LOST – in this hell-palace-Rise – I haven't a clue what to do –

LOST IN THE KITCHENS

Night's arrived. Hallo, night. It was already sunset when we left the big Little Book Room. So, yes, it would be night now. The windows are all high up, and all I could see was fading sky, and now it's black sky, and a couple of stars. Not the Star.

Some lights came on, rather cold, and of course, still and hard.

I'm writing by their glare, sitting on an old table against one wall.

Even before Argul, I haven't been alone much. I used to share a room with Pattoo and Daisy in the House. And a wagon with Hulta girls in the camp. I was alone a lot on the journey with Nemian, and when I was dragged here. But there were always people about somewhere near. And in the Tower, I *wanted* to be alone, get away from the people.

But I'm alone now.

What happened?

Venn went first down the stair, to try it. And he said Grem should come last as back-up to the rest of us. Jotto, Treacle and I in the middle. The cats – J and G and I tried to carry them. They got away though, and rushed down ahead of us. I think they were all right. (Jotto said cats are always coming into the palace, yet always managing to get out again. They can get through tiny holes and they also leap, vastly better than any of us.)

We shared carrying the baggage, and I had my bag. I was also carrying a pillow – but it fell away from me when the stair broke up.

I didn't like that stair. Even though I found it. Maybe it had it in for me. That's silly. But who knows.

At first we moved down with no problems at all, and although no lights came on, Jotto had lit a candle under a glass bulb. It flicked a lot. And the stair started to curve round to the right, and then it was like a corkscrew.

Then it straightened out again and it and we emerged in an open space, with a tile floor below gleaming in the last of the sunset.

'Thank God,' said Venn. He sounded strained.

Perhaps it was his voice – or even some of the cats' voices, since they were sitting in the red pool of light meowing up at us.

The stair *shook itself.*

Treacle and I grabbed for each other but were dashed apart. I fell on to my knees, and little sharp splinters in the stair bit into my knees. (Injury to insult!)

I saw, and couldn't do a thing, Venn and Jotto and their piece of stair going one way – left; and Treacle spinning off on hers to the right.

Grem behind and above me called 'Catch hold of me, lady –' but as I turned and tried to, it was too late and his stair-part was flying him up into the ceiling, which opened to let him through.

And I – I was dropping fast towards the floor – and I

screamed – but the floor too opened wide, and I was dived through, down and forward, into darkness and the smell of old water, moss and rust. The floor above closed up behind me.

When the stairs stopped, I slid off and stood up in blackness. Was it a cellar?

No. As my eyes adjusted, I made out the first line of high windows, their glow just fading.

I stood staring at that till it was all gone.

Then a light popped on.

Somehow it took me ages to realize I was in a sort of kitchen – kitchens – room after room. They must go on, like everything else here, for miles.

Tried to recall what Jotto said about the food. (I apologize for not noting it down properly before, but a lot's been going on.)

Jotto said, I think, the kitchens now make the food, or a lot of it. And he said he meant machines made it, but *in* the kitchens.

These must be the machines.

Up near the ceiling, tanks and bulges and long sprawls of pipes. Which make noises, gurglings and thumps and skinkles.

I don't understand, of course. Maybe you do.

Ven'n – if you ever read this – I don't mean *you*.

The thing is, I don't think anyone ever needs to come all the way down here. You can fetch the food from somewhere else. So the actual kitchen rooms below and around are just unused, and falling apart.

There are old fireplaces, some in walls, some in the centre of floors with hooded indoor chimneys hanging over them, all ready to suck away a smoke that never happens.

There are black stone ovens, and great rusting kettles and pans and cauldrons and spits to turn meat – thick with webs and greasy, ancient dust.

And tables and cupboards and benches and broken bowls and enormous spoons and ladles.

Abandoned.

The smell is overpowering in parts. Of rotted vegetables and cold fats that are perhaps twenty years old. (More?)

A sorrowful, sooty place.

I've even found an old book of recipes, some in other languages, some in mine, some oddly spelled.

'*How to make a cinnamon toad*' – !? Ugh!

I wandered for ages. Water dripped down, and the pipes and vats above made noises. (And also sometimes dripped sticky slimes, so I'll never be able to eat anything from here again. If ever I get the chance.)

It's eerie too. Because of the light and dark, the sounds. Easy to imagine there's something else here with you.

I must find a way out.

So far I haven't found a way out.

I've gone round in circles. I know I passed that big barrel before, oh, about two hours ago.

They don't seem to move, the kitchens. Perhaps they're not allowed to, for fear of disarranging the cooking pipes. Or they do it on the sly, to confuse people trapped here.

I dozed off in this corner. (It's hot, damp and airless.) When I woke, I heard *something moving about*.

It's an echo, of course. Or mice. Rats even. Rats are all right. There's lots of spilled stuff for them to eat.

It didn't sound like a rat or mice.

My imagination.

Something is down here. With me.

Help.

What I'm going to do is find somewhere to hole up until day-break. Some light will come in here from the high windows. I think that may be safer than this false light, which whatever is down here obviously doesn't mind.

I just definitely heard it.

What *is* it?

A sort of fluttering soft rush – and then – almost skittering –

The rush was like wings. Big.

So I wo~~~~~~~~~~

That was where I got up and ran, dragging this book and the bag and everything with me.

I plunged down a corridor and through some more kitchen rooms I may have gone round already. Then I was in a long room more like a very wide passage, with great basins against the walls, and a lot of water was on the floor, splashing up as I ran.

The bad-vegetable smell came strong and repulsive. No lights worked, (thick shadows) only a dim glow filtered through cracks and holes from other places. Things lit up strangely. I kept seeing *eyes*. Perhaps, I thought, they were –

And then I realized I wasn't fighting my way through old dishrags or torn curtains.

Plants grew there, in the half-dark, tall, slender stems and drooping flags of leaves – some of which broke as I pushed by. There were spongy mosses too, I kept treading on them, and huge funguses like dissolving statues – and some of these were luminous.

Despite this, I wasn't prepared for what I saw next.

I'd burst into a *wood*.

That really is what it was. An indoor forest.

There are *trees*, twenty or thirty feet high, their tops crushed against the high ceilings and then spreading and looping over. In places too they've cracked the stone and forced their way through to higher kitchen rooms above. As in the jungle beyond the Rise, creepers rope these trees. There are shrubs that thrust up from the paving. And the funguses, which seemed tall, were now taller, trees themselves, like oaks made of yellowish candlewax. The rest of the vegetation is a pale swimmy green, or oily black . . .

The smell was thicker – yet less horrible. It was more natural, I suppose, earthier.

'Fruits' and 'flowers' grow here too, none very recognizable or tempting. (Fruit like long-fingered gloves, flowers like white spiders – yum.)

Lots of water, spilled from old taps and cisterns, or dripped through by rain.

The food pipes twisted about through all this. I think their leaks have caused these things to grow, plus, too, ancient left-overs, maybe from centuries before – cheeses that have become quaint moulds, or apple cores mixed with other stuff, which may have bred those things like umbrellas with fruit like frogs.

I stood there in the middle of it, uneasy and not liking it, yet impressed. It reminded me of the vegetable forest on the way to Peshamba – where we'd seen the monster –

Then I glanced up and saw, hanging from one of the food pipes, a heavy long thing, some vast knot of creeper or fungus. It had ears. Eyes. The eyes, cool and slitted, were looking at me, still and thoughtful.

Now I could see, it hung upside down from a long hairless tail, which was curled over and over the pipe – the way a bat hangs, though a bat doesn't hang by its tail . . . How big was it? About my size. Bigger . . .

It will just uncurl its tail and spring.

But it didn't. The eyes closed up.

And then I heard that rush-flutter sound, it went directly over my head, and a raw compost-heap-smelling wind fanned me.

Another of them – and it was *flying*.

Not wings. Its stunted little arms were held out and broad flaps of skin stretched between them and its hairy body, carrying it in a long glide, downwards.

They were flying rats.

The flying rat landed near me. It stared at me from grey eyes that didn't reflect enough light to go red. Then it lowered its snout and drank from a pool of rain-water.

I turned my head so slowly I felt my neck creak.

They were all around me. Fumbling about, searching over the mosses for parts they liked to eat. They made the skittery noises when their hair scratched through leaves and fronds.

They must live here, but also, they're all through the kitchens. I'd passed by them. Shadows, smells, eyes. *Not known.*

Why hadn't they attacked me? When would they decide to?

Oh, now, probably. Two or three were edging up on my left, and one was pottering along from over there. Some were smaller or bigger than others. That one looked the size of a large dog. *That* one, when it stood up again on its hind legs, was about as tall as a man.

I wanted to scream my head off.

Instead a thought came into it, sharp and bright. Of the ring in my bag, the topaz.

Properties. What Grem had thought my Hulta ring had, only it hasn't. Had Ustareth's ring got them? Was it, in any way, 'magic'?

I crouched and fished in the bag and scrabbled out the ring. Nearly dropped it in a swamp of water and mud.

It would only fit on my right thumb. I eased it on. The yellow stone gave a flash.

What should I do?

Obviously I'd done it, because, look, the rats had stopped advancing, they were just shambling away.

The ring was burning like a lamp – that flash wasn't from any light, there isn't any proper light just here.

A great gold blaze goes up from Ustareth's ring, and I'm safe.

There's another light, too, though. White. What's causing *that*?

Above, in the mossy wall, a door flies open with a crash. The rats lumber away, not as if afraid. More as if they're shy, irritated, don't want to be disturbed.

'Claidi!'

He leaps down about fifteen feet into all this muck and squelch. It's Venn. He throws his arms round me as if I matter. And I'm clinging to him as if he's my oldest friend. As if he's Argul.

BETWEEN THE SUN AND THE MOON

In the morning, we saw Jotto, and later Treacle, waving up at us from the groves far below. They'd managed to escape back into the gardens.

It was a sunny morning. Always is, here.

The night before, after Venn so dramatically appeared, Grembilard leaned in through the door. There was a strong rope, part of the supplies we'd carted about with us all those days. Grem had attached it to something, and now first I, and then Venn, were hauled up to the place above.

The door was really a window. This part of the kitchen had sunk. A lot of the kitchens anyway lie outside the main building, in various courtyards. This one led up on to a terrace.

The rat-creatures didn't pay much attention. A few glanced up as we closed the window – glad to be rid of us.

'They wouldn't have hurt you,' said Venn.

'No?'

'They're timid, don't like strong lights – even what you call the hard light, though they're fairly used to that. They wander about the lower parts of the Rise at night. Sometimes you see one being chased by a cat.'

'What happens?' I asked dubiously.

'The cat works out the size difference and loses interest. The rat goes off about its own affairs.'

'Did *she* – I mean your mother – ?'

'No, she didn't breed those. They've just got like that by themselves over the past twenty years.'

We camped above the terrace. Dark rustling trees crowded close, grasshoppers chorused, stars winked as faint clouds drifted over. The Star had gone off to the west, and was hidden by angles of the cliff.

Grem fried vegetables over the brazier.

Venn and I were rather embarrassed.

We didn't speak about hugging each other, or sit at all close.

In the red brazier light, he looked now very familiar, but not like Argul at all.

I showed him the topaz ring.

'Yes,' he said, in that cold voice he so often goes back to, 'she said she left that somewhere. I think I was meant to search for it. A little extra test she set me, when she left. I didn't ever bother. I suppose it was in her sleeping-place off the Little Book Room.'

'In a drawer, with some other jewellery.' I explained why I'd taken it, because of Grem's question about my own ring, which made me think Ustareth's one had powers.

'But if it does,' I said, 'why did she leave it behind when she left?'

'Perhaps she was as sick of fiddling about with science as she was of meddling in everything and everyone's lives,' he rasped.

So there was a tense gap, and we ate some of the food. Finally I said, 'But does it have properties – powers –'

'I'd expect so.'

'The stone – the topaz shone out in the kitchen. And the rats backed off. I thought –'

'They backed off from the flash of the ring. Some reflection it caught. I told you, they don't like strong light much.' He was snappy now. So I left it.

It was as if he didn't like me again, or liked me even less

123

because, for a few minutes, he *had* liked me.

Whatever else, I thought I'd better give him the topaz ring. But when I did offer it, he said, 'You keep it. You found it.'

'But –'

To which I got a furious: 'Oh just keep it, Claidi, for God's sake. Why must you keep *on*.' Followed by Venn getting up and stamping off for a walk in the trees, scaring all the grasshoppers into dumbness.

I asked Grem about Treacle and Jotto, and Grem said he thought they would be all right – which of course we now know they are. Then I curled up and tried to sleep.

I hate the way, once you start to know someone, care about them, their behaviour can distress you, even when it's unreasonable and not your fault, even if you were really trying to be careful, tactful.

So, apparently I must care about Venn.

I wish I didn't.

Next day, after we spotted J and T, Grem, who had been out and around, reported that the main library had appeared directly above us, on the 'ninth level', as he said, with the moon and sun towers.

'Yes,' said Venn, who was now being distant and vague, 'it does tend to go there, doesn't it.'

'Generally it then stays in place there for several days,' added Grem. (As if they were talking about something painfully ordinary.)

'I hope you're ready for a long climb, Claidi,' said Venn, now distant, vague, but hearty.

'Not really.'

'Oh, well, that's tough, madam.'

Scowling, I now concluded they'd want me to climb with them up the side of the cliff/building – by ropes – hanging on to the odd statue that stuck out, or wobbly windowsill. And I was getting ready to refuse point blank.

But we walked along around the cliff, through the trees, now and then into a dip and up again. And so reached an *incredible* staircase.

'Before you ask, Claidi, it doesn't move, it's outside the outer wall.'

It was a *mountain* of a stair. I didn't try to count the steps – but looking up and up at it from its foot, I guessed there must be hundreds upon hundreds. Thousands. It was far higher than the highest towers of the House. Perhaps the Wolf Tower.

The stair was also wide, oddly ornate, with carved hand-rails, and marble lions at intervals. (I think they were lions – they were very weathered and mossy.) (Could have been badgers, really.)

Anyway, we started to climb up.

After thirty solid minutes it was getting slightly exhausting, but then there was a broad terrace or landing before the next flight. These landings happen at intervals all the way up. Some even have drinking-water fountains.

The stairs are also crumbly in parts, and cracked where trees have rooted and pushed through. On the seventh landing, I think it was the seventh, when the world seemed already fallen far, far away to a green-blue ring, some big purplish monkeys were thumping about, which threw nectarines at us – until Grem made a loud whooping noise and they fled, leaping off the stairs into space – to catch black-handed on handy neighbouring boughs.

Neither Venn nor Grem seemed tired. *I* tried not to seem

tired, ashamed of my feebleness. I'd thought I'd hardened up a lot, walking and riding with the Hulta. But climbing stairs isn't the same.

We stopped for a longer rest, thank heavens, on the fifteenth landing, or whatever it was. We sheltered from the noon sun under a spreading melon tree. (Grem watered his hair at one of the fountain-taps.)

The view was awe-inspiring but samey. All you could see by now were things tapering away, getting smaller and smaller. The far blue world, the high blue sky.

A large bird flapped across on ragged wings.

Lucky thing.

We got there in the afternoon.

Out of the cliff, these two brown stone towers, not that tall, and without any real distinguishing marks, just a few scattered indigo roof-tiles left. Windows without glass. Shadows running sideways.

'Sun and moon,' said Venn.

'Why?'

'I haven't a single idea. Do you, Grem?'

'No, prince.'

Grem (and Jotto) call him 'prince' as if it's an affectionate nickname.

Wedged between the two disappointing towers was a huge block of building with long glazed windows of coloured glass. It had a vaulted-arched doorway, with its own (yes, more of the things) steps. Guarded by two beasts that were like pigs more than anything.

The Library.

We – I – crawled up the last steps. *They* walked.

It was cool in the vault of the doorway.

Even if it takes off right now, I thought, and goes rambling back down into those kitchens, and won't come out – I don't care.

Venn was looking at the shut door. He said suddenly, 'Try her ring, Claidi.'

Oh, so now we could talk about Her Ring without him going loopy.

'I've put it away,' I said huffily. But I was curious. I walked right up to the door, and started digging in my bag for the topaz.

I hadn't even found it, let alone brought it out, when the door opened. Wide.

Inside looked cool, dust-moted and calm. It had that smell libraries always have, well, so far as I know. Of new paper and old paper, of bindings, and the powders of books.

In the high ceiling was one of those sky-lights, and patterns of sky scattered over the old, dark-tiled floor.

'How did it – ?' said Venn.

I realized the door hadn't been meant to open like that.

'It *recognized* you,' I stated.

'Yes, it does recognize me – but not you. Not even Grem.'

'Well, I probably touched the ring in the bag –'

'You'd have to be wearing the ring, Claidi.'

I thought of the Old Ladies in the House, who had had such authority. Especially wonderful (untrustworthy) Jizania. I said, cool and calm as the library, 'But I'm not. A mystery, then. But what isn't a mystery,' I added in my best Jizania voice, 'is that I'd like some hot tea, now, as soon as possible. Thank you.'

They stared.

I walked on into the library coolness, head high. Secretly frantically hoping they'd hurry and follow, in case anything moved.

And they did. And five minutes later Grem handed me one of the travelling cups full of hot spicy tea.

Really, after what he did, anyway, (reading *this*) I shouldn't have any feelings for Venn, but contempt, distaste. Hatred.

None of that applies. I've almost tried to feel like that. It no longer works.

Instead I feel so sorry for him sometimes I could howl. At other times I want to kill him. And then – he just does something that charms me, turns me round. And then I remember how he held me in his arms when he found me in the kitchens.

Of course, I don't *want* to feel close to him.

It's the old thing, that thing that happened before. I fell for Nemian (who Venn is sometimes *so* like, not to look at, but in his manner. (Even the sudden charm.)) Then I met Argul. And Argul was *right*. He was meant, and *I* was meant.

But now am I just swinging away towards the nearest new attractive (he is) man – a new friend, a new interest. I don't trust myself.

No, I don't feel for Venn the way I feel for Argul – even though I feel I've *lost* Argul, somehow –

No, it's not the same.

And yet –

Oh, Claidi, you absolute hopeless dupp.

Who can I rely on, if I can't rely on myself.

(And now I half want to tear this page out – in case *he* reads it.)

I only want You to know. Well, I do trust *you*. We've never met. Probably never will.

So is that why I trust you? Is that all it can ever mean? So long as one never meets another, one is *safe*?

This isn't getting me anywhere. Except over the page. My 'Journal' – how many pages are left? Just checked. I've filled over three quarters of this book!!!

As I drank my tea, enjoying every gulp, sitting on a marble bench, Venn came up to me.

He stopped before me and bowed low, sweepingly. It made me laugh, and then he smiled, as I've only really seen him do with the others until now.

It's a nice smile. The long mouth and white teeth, and one lower one with a tiny chip off the top. How did that happen?

'Claidi, I apologize for my temper and moodiness. Can you forgive me?' (Just like Nemian.) (But then, not at all like Nemian, that practiced girl-dazzler:) 'It's odd, isn't it, you're the first woman I've ever met, apart from my mother, and Treacle.'

I didn't reply. What could I say that wouldn't cause a problem?

He sat down, quite a way along the bench, gazing, not at me, of course, but up at stacks and stacks of books. There are three galleries, one above another, mounting to the sky-light.

'Claidi. I'd like to try an experiment. I don't want to explain, because that might somehow affect what happens. Would you just do what I ask?'

'You want me to jump out of a window?' I inquired blandly. It was a sort of joke, but he swung round on me.

'Oh – you're joking. I'm sorry. No, no windows. You're not wearing my mother's ring?'

'You can see. It's too big for me, even on my thumb. It's in the bag still.'

'Then, when you're ready, would you stand out on the

floor and ask for a book. The same voice, I think, in which you gave us the order for tea.'

Puzzled, I said, 'Which book?'

'Anything. Something you'd like to read. Something about the City Towers, I suppose.'

I shrugged. I finished my drink and put down the cup. I walked out on to the tiles.

Clearly I announced, 'I'd like a book about the Wolf Tower.' The very *last* thing I'd want in the world, frankly. A pity, that, because presently I got it.

Standing there, I felt the vastness of the library, its height, the shafts of dusty sun. All those books straight-backed like bricks. Others just in paper form, or scrolls rolled on two bits of wood, or tablets of wood *carved* with letters –

Then I heard a ticking begin, all along the shelves. It sounded like dozens of clocks starting up.

I thought of the ghost mice who ate the books, eating more knowledge than he or I could ever manage to read.

Then there was a louder click. All the other ticking stopped. And *then*, down through the air, came drifting, light as a cobweb, this silver thing like a sort of ball of hair. It was all tendrils, and wrapped up in them – a large book in black covers. It was bringing the book from the highest gallery.

The hair-ball laid the book at my feet, detached itself and swam weightlessly off.

Venn picked up the book. He showed me the cover, on which, in dull gold letters and my own, the City's, language, these words: *The Towers*.

He put the book on a nearby table.

Then he just stood there.

Then he came over to me and he grabbed up my left hand.

'It's you – it's *this*.'

'What? Let go of me!'

'Claidi – your *ring*.'

'I'm not wearing it – oh, this one. But this one is a Hulta ring –'

'I know. Claidi, I'm sorry, but remember I read your journal.' (As if I could forget.) 'I know about your ring. Argul gave it you. You told Ironel in the Wolf Tower that it had been your mother's –' Venn hesitated. He said, 'I know you think Ironel wrote to me. She didn't. I've heard of her. That's all. It was Grem who asked you about your own ring. You don't know why. It was because of the dolls in the other house, back across the ravines.'

Totally perplexed, I said, 'Dolly and Whirr and Bow?'

'That's what you called them. You see, they didn't speak, couldn't any more. But when you were there, they started speaking. Even poor old Whirr was trying – that's why he *whirred*.'

'I see,' I said. Didn't.

'There were other things. On the bridge – do you recall when you looked over and down?'

'I'll never forget.'

'The bridge tried to move. It steadied, but for a moment, Grem said he thought you'd both be shaken into the ravine.'

I'd thought that feeling of dizziness was just me.

'The rooms move more, now you're here,' said Venn. 'They always have, but it's worse. The Rose Room, for example, hadn't shifted for about three years. But when you were in it – suddenly it was off, if not very far. As for the first apartment you were in – those yellow rooms – I don't think they'd ever moved, or hardly.'

131

I stood there in my old familiar enchanting pose, my mouth hanging open.

'But, Venn –'

'Then there was the vrabburr – the clockwork one. Claidi, it would probably still have killed you – but it got switched off. I thought then it might be the storm affecting it. But now I think it's your diamond. Yes, I'm damn sure it is.'

'How?'

'Your journal says Argul told you his mother was a scientist. The Hulta called her a magician. The –' he faltered, had the grace to look uneasy, 'the glass thing she gave him that told him how important you were . . .'

I said firmly, before I could even think, 'Argul's mother had nothing to do with the Towers. He never said that much about her, but from what he did, she was great. Wise and kind and funny. He loved her. She died when he was a child.'

'I know. She had to leave him because she died. As opposed to leaving him as a child because she got bored with him, like *my* mother with me. *Ustareth*.' Poison in his voice as he said it. His eyes bleak as a desert. 'Claidi,' said Venn, 'I envy your Argul. In several ways. He's the sort of man I'd have liked to be – heroic – and yet casual. Honest. Good. Brave. *Loved*.'

'Yes,' I said, humble before this praise of my Argul. My lost, almost-husband. Then I said, quite rudely, 'But come off it. Why would anything Hulta have power *here*, in *this* place?'

'Because it's strong,' he said.

I remembered then the white light I'd glimpsed after the light from the topaz, in the kitchens. It hadn't come from the opening window after all. The ring. Mine.

I stared down at it, bewildered.

The ring had powers I'd never known. Could I have learned to manage them, and used it to escape, long before all this entanglement happened?

He was envious of Argul.

Venn said, 'I'll bring that chair over, Claidi. Sit down and read the Tower book for a while.'

'You know, Venn, I really don't want to know *anything* about the rotten ghastly towers.'

'Yes, Claidi, I understand that. But maybe you must.'

'*Why?*'

'I knew you were the daughter of Twilight Star from that flying letter.'

'I may not be her daughter.'

'How can you know, until you find out more? Twilight might be mentioned in that book, at least as a child. I've heard of her. She fell in love with her steward, who'd been a slave.'

'You know that from my book, not –' But he hadn't. Even I hadn't known my father – if he was – had been a slave.

And Venn was saying, 'I know it from my mother, Claidi. She'd heard of *your* mother. I said, she told me stories, before she changed to me. One of those stories was *about* your mother. I know you're younger than me – when I was two you weren't even born, were you? But Twilight and your father – they were together for some time before you arrived. I can't remember his name. She must have said. But she did say this, Twilight was strong, clever – different. That's why Grem and I thought Twilight might have made your ring . . . Ustareth used to admire her. Ustareth said Twilight "Broke the rules". I can recall Ustareth saying that, and her eyes were bright. *She broke the rules, thank God for her.* That's what she said.'

He glanced at me. Away.

'Claidi, a daughter might be like her mother. What did *you* do?'

I was trembling.

Slowly I answered, 'I broke the rules.'

Before I start, I've written everything up. Mainly to put off opening the black book. *The Towers*.

Scared.

Afraid of my ring, too. My beautiful ring that Argul tried to give me in Peshamba, gave me in the City.

Argul's mother was Zeera, a real Hulta name. And she *was* Hulta, wasn't she? When I was with them, a couple of the younger women had that name too, called after her, I think.

Somehow it's disturbing to think that she died when Argul was ten, just as Venn's mother vanished when he was nine. Even so, Argul knew Zeera all those ten years. Venn only knew Ustareth before she changed towards him, stopped loving him. I keep thinking about this. Even while I'm getting ready to read this black book.

Before leaving me, going off into the depths of the library, I think he said to look for something himself – Venn said this:

'Strange, Claidi. Where the library is now, between the sun and moon towers. There used to be an old expression, *she* used to use it. Being between the sun and the moon. It meant being between two vital things. Having to make a decision, a choice.'

As I am? Between my freedom and Their Law? Between my future and my past?

Between Argul . . . and Venn?

I just now opened the black cover of the book, and the first thing I saw was a printed drawing. Of a huge tower.

Not like these. Like the City Towers.

Like the Wolf Tower I thought I'd never see again.

Have I learnt anything?

I've sat here, more or less, reading for hours, almost all the long second half of the afternoon.

There are two bathrooms with the library, (old cracked baths on rusted gilded feet) cupboards stuffed with ink pencils (I took one) shut wooden boxes, and brooms.

There's a kitchen still attached that goes into a rundown yard . . .

It's silly to start describing all that. Basically I still don't understand much about the Towers.

Though not very old, the black book is one of those books that read like this: 'And thereinunto they have done that which verily it please them that they do muchly.' (!) (Sigh). No, I'm not myself muchly pleased. So my dread has turned to exasperation.

Venn has vanished. There's a high roof-terrace or something. I think he's gone up there.

I wish he'd stayed to help with this.

I'm glad he's gone away.

I'll read a bit more.

The Towers weren't there first. The Families were.

I remember those names, which I see again here. Wolf, Vulture, Tiger, Pig or Boar. And once there was a Raven Family and a Raven Tower, but they were destroyed.

Historically, the Families fight together. Then they pal up. They make alliances, swearing eternal friendship, and sons and daughters of one Family or Tower marry into another, to tie everyone together neatly. But then another quarrel starts, generally over something mind-searingly unimportant, and they're off again, using cannon to blow each other's Towers in pieces.

They were always fighting. In the end they were sick of it, and the harm they'd done to each other and themselves.

So then they thought of the Law.

The Law isn't the same everywhere. I'd already realized that. At the House the Law was that we had endless stupid rituals which *had* to be followed.

According to the black book there are other cities, other grand houses or palaces – some called things like the Residence, or Sea-View. The Families, in one form or another, are scattered about through these places. They all have some type of the Law, which must be followed. But not all of them call it Wolf Tower Law. Despite the fact that the Wolf Tower seems to have ended up the most powerful, and the WT Families are therefore the most important. (I remember the authority Nemian had for Jizania, once she knew who he was.)

If I've got it right, the Law, in whatever form, is there to use up the Families 'fighting spirit'. Turn it away from war and argument. The Law seems to have been invented to stop them having the time or energy to cause trouble otherwise.

But of course, they do cause trouble. The Law itself causes trouble. (I'm truly afraid now I won't have stopped it properly, in the City, and even if I did, only in that one place.)

The black book doesn't say that the Law is, ultimately, just as cruel and senseless as war-making. The black book is all for the Law. *This cunning and most absolute Notion* is what the book calls it.

I don't know. I don't want to write any more about it,

and there isn't much more. It just goes on and on, endless histories of these impossibly terminally-useless mighty lords, ladies, princes and princesses, flomping about, basking in how fantastic they are.

But. I did finally find something. It's two Family trees, tables of who married who — the 'm' means married, so far as I can gather. And what children were then born.

I'll just copy it in.

Ironel (Vulture Tower) — M — Khiur Novendot (Wolf Tower)

A Daughter: Alabaster — M — A Prince of the Wolf Tower

A Son: Nemian

A Daughter: Ustareth — M — A Prince of the Vulture Tower

A Son: Venarion (born Palace of the Rise)

(Something I noticed from this one at once was how they hadn't bothered to name two of the three fathers, only Ironel's husband, (Ironel married!!!!!) and the two sons.) Does Venn know she's his granny? And Nemian — is Venn's cousin! No wonder they sometimes have nearly the same voice. And Ustareth is Ironel's *daughter* — one more unbelievable thought.

But then I saw the second Family tree, and my heart jumped and hit its head on the underside of my chin.

Jizania Tiger (Tiger Tower) — M — Wasliwa Star (the House)

A Daughter: Twilight Star

THE ROOF

'No thanks. I really don't want anything else to read just yet,' I said, as Venn held out a slim pale-covered book the moment I emerged on the library roof.

I'd climbed up the stair from the galleries and now I was there, I stretched, shook my hair about, glad to be in the fresh air again. The sun was low. It would be a spectacular sunset from up here – the highest point now, from the look of it, of the whole Rise. I could even see the waterfall a huge distance off, at the other end of the cliff, shimmering like a curtain of lights.

'This is different.'

'It's a book, Venn. That other book has probably put me off reading for ever.'

'What did you learn?'

Cagily I said, 'Not much. Couldn't understand most of it.' Then, 'It did list Ironel Novendot.' When he didn't react I announced, 'She's your grandmother, Ustareth's mother.'

Perhaps I shouldn't have been so blunt – nor surprised when he laughed.

'*Is* she? What horrors I've been spared, never meeting her.'

'Did Ust – did your mother talk about her?'

'She must have, a little. Never as her mother. I'm just going on your own intense description of the Old Lady.'

'Right. Of course.'

'Did it list your own mother?'

'As I keep saying, *if* she was. Yes.'

I was sullen, and half turned from him. He knows too much about me. He's got no right to know *this*. Which is unreasonable. He'd only have to fetch the black book himself.

'Was it of any help?'

'No.'

'That's very positive, Claidi.'

'It's very true.'

'Try this, then.'

'I don't want to. What is it?'

'Look and see.'

Nosiness, my strongest characteristic?, won over everything else. I took the pale book.

The instant I opened it, I saw it was another Journal. Not like mine. This one was hardly filled, mostly only a few lines or paragraphs here or there, then blank pages. One line was *Why am I here?* That *did* catch my eyes. Another: *I'm tired of waiting*.

Then a full page. I couldn't read a lot of it – the light was going, but also the handwriting . . . and he'd dared go on about mine.

But, it was a woman's handwriting, I thought. Who was this?

Over the page: *I shall go tomorrow.* And then nothing. The rest of the book, empty.

Ustareth?

Then I tried quite hard to read what she'd written. She was impatient, you could tell. Her writing was educated – she was a princess, a lady – but untidy and scrawly with anger and hurry – or perhaps tiredness.

I'd sat down, my back against the high railing around the roof.

I didn't copy down what she wrote – there was too much anyway. I'll just say what I found out.

She'd been sent here by someone she didn't name – Ironel? Or the weird and worrying 'We' . . . She'd had no choice. Nor in her marriage. It was the *Law*. Her husband was called, I think, Narsident Vulture-Ax, from the fed-up scribble. (As I often do, she soon reduced him to NV.)

In the unhappy, forced marriage, she made 'scenes', so they'd sent her off here alone, to do 'something'. She was, at the time, pregnant with Venn. Imagine that sea-crossing – She said she had to travel by sea, they didn't trust the balloons over water. (I'd always rather wondered about that, why they'd put me off on to a ship.)

She didn't say much about anything. She didn't complain, although now and then she wrote some simply explosive swear-words, (typical of royalty). But though you couldn't always read the rest, *these* words were always printed carefully, even sometimes ornamented with curlicues . . . I have to admit, I smiled once or twice.

The birth of Venn was by itself in the middle of one page. It said, 'Free at last. I had the boy.' (She knew he'd be a boy?) 'My mechanical servants were useful, better than those idiots in the Tower.'

That was all.

I thought of Venn, reading this.

As he may have done, I scanned the next pages, which obviously covered months, years, for any comment on him at all. There was only one. 'He's intelligent'. That was it. I suppose she did mean Venn?

Had she *ever* loved him or been interested in him?

She hadn't wanted him.

This is all rather – I don't like putting this down. In a way, he's let me pay him out for reading my own book, letting me see this.

From what I could make out, no one was at the Rise but for her, and her servants, though Families of the Towers had been living there in earlier times. There was one mention of local people – 'Otherlanders' – arriving on a sort of visit. She made no comment.

On one page there was a beautiful, involved description of a new plant she'd somehow grown, a mix of a lilac and a pear, that produced fragrant purple fruit. She cared about that. Then again, three pages later, she just says, 'Mauve thing died.' So. (Where are her other notes on her endless experiments – the vrabburrs and dolls, the moving rooms – ?)

But there was one long passage which may have been why he gave me the book to read. It isn't about him, or about her. It's about what she was sent here to do, twenty years or so ago.

I read it, and thought she'd made it up, or was talking in some clever way that wasn't meant to be taken seriously.

But then it seemed she did mean it, so she was mad.

Then again – there are things here – if I hadn't seen them, I'd have thought they were all lies.

He was leaning on the railing a long way off across the roof, looking out towards a deepening red sunset.

'Venn . . . can I ask you? This stuff about *creating* the jungle – these things about plants and animals being bred here, and then taken away to the Towers and Houses and so on – as if this was a sort of farm, or workshop, for the benefit of the places back over the sea – It isn't true, is it?'

'Yes,' he said.

The short sunset was already ending, and I'd missed most of it. I'd really wanted to see it from up here, too – after all, the library might not still be up here tomorrow, or we might not. (We won't be.)

'But – she seems to say they sent her here to *make* the jungle – where there was mostly a *desert waste* –'

'Yes. That's why they sent her. Apart from punishing her, or course, for irritating them all.'

'How could she do that? *Make* a jungle?'

'How could she do any of it? Think of the animals. Think of Jotto.'

'But the jungle-forest is *immense* – and natural.'

'She was very clever and she worked very hard. And she had lots of machines she herself invented, to help her. Planting and sowing, working out systems to water everything or bring rain – she did most of it in the first two years. Then, because of how she'd arranged it all, the jungle grew and spread *itself*. I can remember bare places, long areas of sand, even when I was seven or eight, that grew over, filled up. I used to like all that, before I got used to it.'

The red was maroon now, and going out. Soaked up by the vast sponge of the *jungle*. In the afterglow, a white ghost came wheeling through the sky below, on two wide sails.

Venn held out his arm, and the owl veered slowly in and alighted on him, folding its vast ghostly wings. 'Hallo, owl,' he said to it, and it turned its head, that way they do, almost all around, like a stopper in a bottle, to look at him.

'Even the owl,' said Venn.

'What do you mean?'

'You think he's quite real, don't you?'

'The owl is a doll?'

'Yes, Claidi. Once a month, Jotto or Grem or I undo a little panel – look, under the feathers, there – and oil him. He's two years younger than me. She made him for me and gave him to me that day, when she said, 'You're two, now.' The day she changed.'

'But – he *eats* things!'

'But he's not supposed to.'

The owl settled. It closed its eyes and all the light went from the sky.

'I missed the sunset, reading her journal,' I lamely said.

'Never mind. You'll see the Star come up in a minute. I wanted you to see that, Claidi, from here. Let's go over to the east side of the roof.'

Down and down, the miles and miles and miles of now-dimming forest. The huge, sky-touching trees and knitting of creepers that cover and devour everything – roads, statues – vegetable lushness and life.

Ustareth made all that. Can it be possible?

Venn must hate his father, too, this unknown prince with the ugly name – *Narsident*, from the Vulture Tower.

'She doesn't,' I said, 'say much about her experiments. And – did she have a special room in the Rise where she worked?'

'No,' he said. I was going to say, *Then where*? but he said, 'Come here, Claidi. The Wolf Star's coming up. I want you to see.'

'I don't like your Star.'

'You said. It isn't mine.'

We stood there.

There was a gleam, in the distance, and down. I thought it was a lake or something I'd never been high enough to see before, catching the rays of the Star – which I couldn't yet see either.

But the glow got unbearably fiercer and whiter, until it was almost blinding.

'You're not missing that, are you, Claidi-Claidis?'

'What is it?'

'What do you think, madam?'

'Something's on fire – white fire.'

'Almost.'

And then the scorching blaze began, inch by inch – in fact mile by mile – to *rise*. Up out of the forests. Up into the eastern air. Up and up. It was clear of the land and into the sky, now.

'The Star –' I said.

He said nothing.

'But Venn – it didn't come over the horizon how a star would –'

'No.'

'It came up from the jungle!'

'Ustareth made that too,' he said. Already the blue-white glare had drained his face of any colour. 'It's called the Wolf Star, but it isn't a star.'

'What *is* it?'

We watched as *It* went on rising into the height of the east, and at the same time drew nearer.

'I don't know, Claidi. But she used to go there to do her work. It's on the earth by day, on a high plateau in the jungle. By night, up it goes, as you see, moves round the sky, returns in the morning before sunrise. She'd be gone for days. I mean, when I was an infant, and the rest of the time she was with me. Days and nights. So she must also have travelled in it. Up *there*. It goes much higher than a balloon, do you realize that, Claidi?'

'Yes.'

'She never took me to see it. Let alone sail in it. But she talked about it, once or twice. It sounded magical. It's only mechanical. All the mechanical controls are in it that make the Rise – how shall I say – *run*. Things to do with the food machines, even the way we use the waterfall for power. The rooms moving, that too. All are somehow worked – from up there.'

'Do you think – does she *live* on the Star?' I gasped.

'She might have. But no, I think eventually she just arranged it to work by itself, like everything else. I think when she left she went far away. As far as she could get.'

Our heads were tilting back, to watch the Star rise ever higher.

The owl, turned to silver, slept. Only – it didn't. Dolls don't.

(I'd puzzled how he'd trained it to steal my book. Obviously, he'd only had to *set* it.)

'Why are you telling me all this, Venn?'

'You break rules,' he said, dreamily. 'You break machines, don't you?'

He meant I'd broken, defaced the dice in the Wolf Tower. I went cold.

'Why would I?'

We were looking at each other. Straight into each other's eyes.

'To find your way home. To get back to your Hulta people. And *him*.'

HOW WE LEFT THERE

We got out of the library soon after, went down the great stair to the first landing. The black book was left behind for the hairy machines to replace. Venn brought the other book, hers.

On the way down, the owl flew round him twice. Then flew away.

Grem cooked supper on the landing. Fireflies appeared from nowhere, as if attracted to the brazier flames.

'We'll have some sleep. Get up and go all the way down when the Star comes back over, before dawn. An early start. Then we can arrange things. For the journey.' Venn. He was very organized. In control. It was all his plan now, and Grem and I were just being swept along. Perhaps that was fine for Grem.

'I want to talk about this,' I said.

'Do you? What's to talk about?'.

'All of it.'

'Claidi, you've never struck me before as painstakingly slow and thorough.'

'Haven't I?'

'All right. Say what you want.'

'Well, thank you.' So I said what I wanted. I said that he seemed to think we could set out from the Rise, go through the jungle, find the Star, (handily parked on some plateau or other) nip into it, get me to smash it up – because I'm good at that?

'Is *that* what you thought I meant?'

'Isn't it?'

'Not quite.'

'If,' I said, 'the Star is some sort of sky-ship(?) and has machines in it that somehow work the palace, won't they be difficult to damage? Besides which I don't see myself doing that, somehow. In the Wolf Tower I destroyed – tried to – the dice and records of names – for a purpose. But if the things on her ship-star are broken, what will happen here?'

'The rooms will stop moving about, at the very least.'

'The food machines may stop too – the light. Even the water may be affected –'

'How housewifely you are,' he jeered.

'*Human* is the word you're looking for.'

'Oh my.'

'No, Venn. What about Grem and Jotto and Treacle – and all these animals that come and go –'

'Not everything we eat comes from machines. Haven't you noticed the gardens are bursting with fresh fruit and veg. There are even tea bushes, and Treacle is an expert at picking and drying the leaves. Jotto is a master-cook, despite anything he says. Even I can bake bread. As for the animals, they really don't need us. They're terribly good at surviving *without* people.'

I said, 'What about the little animals in the enclosure?'

'You thought they were cute? They get out all the time. Jotto goes mad finding them. They're happy in the gardens, and I've seen them band together and frighten off a monkey. People – well in fact, people rather cramp an animal's style.'

I decided not to hurl my plate at him. (Grem came quietly and took it from me anyway.)

'As for the light, we have lamps and candles. As for the water, most of the taps run straight off the waterfall. Apart from that, none of us might want to stay.'

'I see. So after I ruin the ship-thing for you, I'm to take myself off *home*, as you put it, though I don't see how. While the rest of you bounce away in other directions. Is that it?'

He laughed, that way he does, low and soft. Somehow it ended my anger.

'You haven't seen what I mean, Claidi. I explained all wrong.'

'I haven't, no. No?'

'I didn't really mean smash the Star machines. Just – break their routine. Use them. Think about it. Apart from anything

147

down here, what does the Star actually do?'

'Rises and goes down.'

'And crosses the sky. Both ways.'

I thought. 'Oh,' I said.

'Yes, Claidi. Perhaps it's possible to make it go another way – any way you want.'

'Across the sea –'

'Why not?'

'How?'

'I don't know. We have to get there, get into it, and see.'

'*We* have to.'

He sat back, clasping one knee. His legs are long. Nemian used to sit like this, looking like this. And Argul. Probably lots of men, and women, do. Why do there only seem to be these three men in the world?

'Well, Claidi, if I asked you to stay here, with me, you wouldn't want to, would you?'

A long silence.

The fireflies had gone. Down in the jungles mother made, monkeys abruptly began hooting, as they do now and then at night, scaring you witless.

Then again, the long silence.

'I didn't think,' I said, 'I had a choice.'

'I've shown you you may have. *She* didn't want to be here. They made her. She left. You're the same.'

'Then you –'

'Oh, I won't go with you. To the Star, yes. The country down there is full of tigapards, and all the rest of it: her bred animals; the *real* vrabburrs – you'll need me to help you reach the Star. No one else. I wouldn't risk Jotto or Treacle in that mess. I shan't ask Grem.'

'You're saying you'll see me to the ship – if it is.'

'And then I'll come back here.'

I looked at him under my lids. He was staring up at the sky above, from which the star had by now moved away.

'You said you might all leave.'

'We might. But not with you. We – I – don't belong in Claidi's world. Though . . . you could have been welcome in mine.'

A rush almost like tears closed my throat so I couldn't or didn't speak.

I thought, This is crazy. If we do this, we'll be eaten alive by vrabburrs, or something else his awful mother made or bred. Or we won't find the Star at all. Or we won't be able to get into it.

We'll end up back here, both of us.

So it's unwise to start dreaming myself back with Argul. Or being afraid of this good-bye. Afraid of something I don't understand and can't recognize.

I couldn't stay with Venn. Not if I have the choice. Argul is the one. He always will be the one.

And yet –

'There's a firefly in your hair,' Venn said in a hushed voice.

I became aware of the green–gold spark only in the instant it zig-zagged away.

When I looked up, he said, in the cold arrogant voice, 'And the rings might work against any dangers. Hers or yours. So let's stop *chattering* and get some sleep.'

It's so sudden, happening so fast. Too fast.

They've waved us off. They did wave. Jotto had his favourite chicken under one arm for comfort, a smart chicken with white stripes.

I feel as if I've lived here a long time. Not a month or so – many years.

All such a *hurry*.

I wish it hadn't been. I wanted to go on that walk again, that long one with the trees with blue flowers, and that pool with the big fish, and the hydrangeas . . . I liked that game Jotto taught me – did I ever say – with the little painted squares. And Treacle watering the pots of flowers from her eyes, which, saying farewell, were *dry*, though she looked sad and stern. Perhaps, if she really does ever cry, her real tears *have* to be made of *nothing* –

She's frightened for him.

I've never asked where they're from, Treacle and Grem. The children of Ustareth's slaves – or of free people from the land about, which was then a waste. How did she make them have leaf-hair, watering-can eyes? How? (And how could she?)

Grem kept flatly saying he'd come with us. Was refused. And Jotto offered, very bravely, because you could see he was appalled at the thought of the jungles.

I liked living in the pavilion. I did. And the statue of the porcupine I found in the back-room. Jotto and I had planned to move it out under that big tree. He says he will, anyway.

I'll never see it there.

I'll never see any of it again.

The gardens are beautiful. They looked wonderful in the dawn as we came down off the stairs and then the terraces, into them. Mists of trees floating in fogs of light –

Seven cats washing each other in the shade.

The Gardener cleaning out a bird-bath, turning his back on us. He certainly doesn't care if any of us stays or goes.

Those little animals, the tiny ones, hippos and rabbits,

pouces and geese and tigapards. We could have had a last dinner, played with them. Or just gone and seen them in their enclosure.

And the waterfall, it was so splendid –

I'd have liked to go and look at it at the other end of the Rise. The sound I've got so used to that I don't hear it. It's going to be odd, really not-hearing it.

And the rat-beasts in the kitchens, poor old things.

And just being able to reach up and pick a ripe peach or orange, whenever I wanted.

And all the coloured windows glowing from the cliff in the dusk after the swift sunsets.

And the infuriatingly blinding light of the Star.

The Star.

Stop it, Claidi. Just stop.

I'm just nervous about going into the jungles again. Especially now I know about them. And what's in them.

No, that's not it.

We'd packed. I didn't have much, and offered to carry more, but also got refused. (No one can refuse like Venn!)

Treacle brought me some different clothes to wear, smooth silky trousers and a tunic, high boots because of snakes, (which until now I've only admired and not bothered about.)

He has a rifle. And bullets.

He took her ring, too, the topaz. Put it on, (it fits him, perhaps she made it for him, anyway.) Then he looked uncomfortable, kept pushing it and turning it as if he wanted to drag it off.

Jotto brought us food in little waxed paper boxes, and

water-bottles. I did take some of those.

My bag feels heavy. Like my heart. Oh what a line, worthy of that awful writer Lady Jade Leaf, at the House.

They were on the lawn under the tree with flowers, where the porcupine may go, when they waved.

Grem embraced Venn. Then Jotto embraced him. Then Jotto embraced me. Jotto looked tearful, and like Treacle he can't actually cry. (*She* might have thought of that. If she gave him the emotions, she might have made him able to express them.)

Treacle turned one solemn good-bye cartwheel. Today her knickers were scarlet with blue dots. This almost seemed the saddest thing of all.

I hated coming here. I was terrified and raging. At least *I* didn't cry as we marched away.

And I'll be alone with him now, as never before, in the depths of the jungle-forest.

Her forest.

HER FOREST

Trees. Shrubs. Shadows.

Glittery strings of water falling from high rocks smothered in vines.

Flowers without colour or scent.

Flashes of parakeets high up in the canopy.

It's the way it was, coming here. There's no point going on about it again. The only difference is knowing she planted it and made it grow. It was her talent for science that enabled everything to grow so quickly, so lushly. And so tall.

This used to be a desert waste. Like the one that

surrounded the House. Dust and buried ruins and mostly poisonous wells. And now, it's this.

Trees, shrubs . . .

Glittery strings of water . . .

And vast silences, now the waterfall thunder has died away.

I'd thought we'd be awkward together, or I would, but while we're on the move, of course, that doesn't come into it.

Venn has to hack our way through, and so do I as much as I can. The faintly-shining path I'd seen before keeps on, descending from the Rise, now coiling to left or right, around things, and in parts smothered. It's exhausting. When we rest during the day, we sometimes just drink some water and then fall asleep. Neither of us is used to this sort of thing. No proper stamina.

Often at night, though, we can't sleep. The Vast Silences get shattered all the time by yowling monkeys, or deer (he says they're deer) abruptly crashing by through the undergrowth. Once something leapt right over us, a living arc with legs and *eyes*.

Tigapards prowl. We hear them. They don't come near the fire, or do the rings keep them away? (I've recalled that time on the beach, after I'd just got off the ship, the tigapard which behaved so oddly, and never came near me.) So, my ring is as powerful as Ustareth's? This still seems wrong. How could it be. Was Zeera herself as powerful as Ustareth??? She didn't sound that way. And Zeera was kind. She *looked after* people.

We did see a vrabburr, the very first morning.

We were on a steep part, and I'd got tangled in a creeper, slashing at it, and Venn said '*Ssh.*' I had the sense to realize it wasn't him being moody again.

When the vrabburr appeared it was a few yards away – that area was abnormally clear, or we wouldn't have seen it.

Vrabburrs kind of lope. Very unevenly, because the front paws are so much shorter than those great heavy back legs. It fallollopped across the path, and shouldered, if you see what I mean, through into the rest of the jungle.

Hadn't scented or seen us, or whatever. He said, 'It must have been clockwork, that one.' So maybe the clockwork ones can't even scent or see you – unless you're very obvious and close. I haven't asked. I'd rather not know, really.

Anyway, he says – now we're out here, so perhaps he's only lying to reassure me – that the vrabburrs are less in numbers now. The clockwork ones run down (why didn't he leave that other one run down, then, why wind it up again, if they're dangerous?) and the real, bred ones have spread out into the farther jungles. Lucky old farther jungles.

As I say, at night we stay awake a lot.

We sit, or lie, a great space apart across the fire, usually turned away and not looking at each other, and we talk.

Argul and I used to talk for hours when we were alone, but not yards apart. And even our most serious discussions were full of jokes. We didn't seem to talk much either about the past. It was sometimes about that evening, or that day, but more often about tomorrow. Next month.

Venn and I talk mostly about the past.

'I remember that tree over there, Claidi. Do you see? Yes, that palm. She used to bring me to look at it. I was about one and a half.'

'You remember a lot from when you were very young. Most people don't.'

'That's because most of my life happened to me before I

154

was two.' I digested *that*, and he said, 'To start it was only a little plant, the palm, in the middle of nothing. All this was bare. Sand, with just a bit of water welling up round a stone. But when she brought me next, the palm was already taller than I was. And there were other things growing everywhere. All about thirty feet high. Look at it now. Tall as the sky. I thought it was magic, what she could do. I still do, in a way. Well, in a way, it is.'

Odd. I could just picture Zeera at that moment, with *Argul* as a little boy, standing by her, and the palm tree growing. 'So you think she did *some* good then?' I said.

'Oh yes. Great good. If I think about her now I'm an adult, well, she must have been very unhappy. I remember something in her book, the one I showed you – did you read this bit? About how she quite liked Narsident – my father – when they first introduced him to her.'

'I don't remember reading that, I couldn't read parts –'

He opened the larger bag and produced the book (he's brought it with him). I wished he hadn't. Her book makes me uncomfortable. But I suppose, once he found it in the library . . . didn't he ever look before? . . . it's all he's got left of the real Her.

Anyway, he read me this thing about how she thought at first her husband was handsome and noble, and then found out he was awful and she hated him. But it was too late by then. Then Venn read a sentence in which she added that she thought everyone should have some way of telling if the person they were attracted to was really right for them.

Of course, I thought at once of Zeera's glass charm she gave to Argul. The thing he'd looked at when he met me. The way he could be sure *we* were right, that he truly did want *me*. (Had Venn thought of that too?)

155

Strange.

Venn sighed and said, 'She wasn't so bad, you know. I'm not fair to her.'

'Well, she left you.'

'She wasn't so bad. At least, not to other people. She helped the local people, Otherlanders, she called them. If they got ill, or their crops failed. They'd bring people to the Rise with a broken arm . . . She'd make them well. Or – she did that until she changed. After that, she wouldn't see them. She'd hardly see *me*. She preferred her mechanical dolls.'

(I heard Argul saying to me, '. . . My mother told me about Peshamba.' Peshamba, the city with mechanical dolls.

And, 'She knew such a lot. Herbs and chemicals.')

I said, 'Venn –'

'Yes, I know. She was a terrible person.'

'I was going to say, in some ways she sounds – like Argul's mother.'

'I know. I caught that when I read – your journal. What you wrote that he said about her. And about Peshamba, too. My mother could almost have invented and made Peshamba.'

'But it's coincidence. Zeera was Hulta. And anyway she was there with them, long before Ustareth left the Rise. Argul's eighteen, two years younger than you –'

'No, three,' Venn corrected me. (Hadn't realized Venn was as old as that –)

'Three, then. But that would make *you* three when Argul was born – and she didn't leave here until you were nine. Is it possible somehow, later, she and Zeera could have met?'

'If they had, Ustareth would have thought Argul's mother was a barbarian.'

'And Argul's mother would have thought Ustareth was a tronker!' I flared.

156

End of discussion.

Although Venn hates her himself, he doesn't like anyone else to insult Ustareth.

It's quite difficult trying to see to write by dying firelight.

Actually, last night, (after the deer or whatever leaped over us) I asked Venn about the two men who abducted me, Hrald and Yazkool. It was to make conversation, really.

Venn said he didn't know them. So I asked what Grem had thought. Venn then said Grem hadn't seen them, they'd been gone when he crossed to the house.

Something in that seemed weird, and I thought back to that morning. Bellowing monkeys, smashed plates on the terrace and upturned chair, a breakfast started and left. How I'd thought H and Y had been thrown into the gulf. 'They left in a hurry then. I thought you paid them?'

'Oh, I'd sent a courtesy payment, with Grem. He didn't see them so he just brought it back.'

'Why did they rush off?'

It seemed he wasn't going to answer. He didn't, then.

Then, somewhere in the dark I heard him say, 'Those two ruffians. It's possible something carried them off. It occurred to me when I saw what you wrote about it.'

I'd been drifting to sleep. This woke me up and no mistake.

'I don't know if I should tell you,' he said, 'I know you'll get anxious.'

'And my life otherwise is such a serene sea of calm.'

'Claidi, you *deserve* to be told. Yes, something may have taken them. They were on the roof-terrace. Something like this happened once before.'

'When? Who?' I gabbled.

157

'A servant of my mother's. He was old, and very gentle. Heepo. He used to talk to me a lot after she stopped talking, find me things to do that I liked.'

'And – ?'

'Well, Claidi, when I was about seven, Heepo was out on a high balcony of the room where I was playing. It was noon. A sort of shadow flicked over the light. I didn't bother for a moment, and then I looked up. Nothing was there. And nor was Heepo. I thought he'd gone out of the room, not telling me, which wouldn't have been like him. I looked for him, couldn't find him. Then Grem looked too, and Treacle. I even got my courage together and went and disturbed Ustareth. She didn't say much. Just, Yes, never mind, or something, as if I'd lost a toy. But we never saw Heepo again.'

'You're saying something *swooped* down and took him off the balcony – without even a cry –'

'Without anything. Just that flick of shadow, which I didn't look at. It was too fast, you see. It was just *there* – then gone. He didn't have time to call. And neither did those two – Hrald and Yaz-the-fool. But the monkeys must have seen something and it scared them badly.'

'What *was* it?'

'All our talks circle round Ustareth. She bred a lot of birds here. Perhaps some very large bird, very fast, predatory.'

So, one more delightful menace to look out for.

I'm so *pleased* I never knew this at the Rise. All those high places I sat in the sun, those landings on the great outside staircase – the roof of the library!

The path stopped this afternoon.

We were far down the cliff, jungle looming above and

falling away in front, never able to see far. Mist of blue distance through leaves.

When it went, we searched for a while. But this time the path hadn't been covered by vines or broken up by bushes. It wasn't there any more. No more path.

'She used to bring me this way,' he said, angrily. 'And the path went on much further. Right to the base of the cliff and then there was a deer-path –'

He was irrationally furious – with rational good reason. I sat under a tree while he raved.

Then he growled at me, 'Come *on* then.'

Whenever things don't go right, I get this impression all this is my fault. The journey we're having to make, I mean. But really, I never wanted to do this. I'd have gone the other way, if I'd made the choice. The way I was brought here. Used the road, tried to find a place on the coast with ships –

But now it all seems: Well I'm doing this for *you*. So the least *you* can do is keep up/cut a way through faster/not want to rest or to have a drink of water.

Or a pause for lunch.

I'd been thinking, at least he talks to me now like a normal person. Huh!

He's strong after all. He kept tearing on, kicking and chopping stuff out of the way. Birds flew up screaming.

Finally, late in the afternoon, I said, 'I can't go any farther without a rest. I'm sorry.'

And he heaved a great sigh. 'Oh all right, all right. In about ten minutes, once we get down to that wild fig tree.'

It doesn't seem any harder without the path, anyway.

He's gone to sleep, leaning on the fig tree.

We've been here three hours. Lost all the time we gained in the mad scramble.

When the Star comes over, even through all these leaves jagged pieces of light drop through.

I mean, I'd never have chosen to go this way, towards her Star.

Breaks in the tree-line. Looking into the forest below he showed me a *lynx* – a small, cat-like creature, tufted ears, very pretty and not friendly. Later on, as we were trying to find a way down, I saw another lynx – only it wasn't. This one (it had a spotted coat, grey eyes gleaming in the jungle-dusk) was a jaguar.

I asked him, after we *got* down, and when we eventually made our 'camp' for the night, if the animals at the House, the lions and hippos, Jizania's blue bird – if originally they came from here.

'Possibly,' he said.

He doesn't say much at the moment. Even showing me the lynx was: 'Look. There's a lynx.'

He's in his Nemian-phase. The non-charming one.

It's when he's in an Argul-phase . . . not that he's like Argul, just looks like him, is efficient, leaderly, funny and helpful, like Argul – that's when I really should be most wary.

I should be glad he's being a pain, glad I don't like him or feel close to him. At the moment.

We're all the way down the cliff. It towers behind us, a dark green living wall. (The Rise is invisible.)

We march (stumble, hack, claw) a way onward.

Saw another of those strange old statues today, we passed quite near it. It seemed to be of a bear, like the one near

Peshamba. Not really the same sort of bear, though. It was carved very shaggy and had huge teeth, with flowers growing between them, as if it were eating them. But I suppose they, or their bush, were really eating the statue, rotting it away.

He has been THE END all today.

I shouted at him, Why had he made us do this?

He shouted, Because he knew I couldn't stand it at the Rise, kept on 'whining' I had to get back to my 'people' (the way he said it) these 'barbarians', and to my 'barbarian chieftain love'.

I yelled that my BCL was worth ninety times ninety of any City-bred fool of a prince.

We both ended up suddenly laughing. Both apologized.

But it isn't comfortable.

The worse thing is feeling we are never going to get anywhere.

I mean, we can't see where we are or where we're going, although there are sometimes breaks in the trees, glades where he takes a 'reading' from the sun or stars.

We saw a ruined building yesterday, near sunfall. Crimson and yellow parrots were flying round it; they have nests in the broken roofs. He said it was a temple. It had been here since the time of the waste.

A temple to what?

'To God, in one of God's many forms,' he sweepingly replied. 'I think this one was a parrot.'

We did look in at the great open front, but lots of the temple had fallen in, pulled down by creepers. A white monkey sat claw-combing his fur.

* * *

161

An abandoned overgrown village. We more or less fell right into it. A mat of moss and vines gave way – and we nearly dropped into a sunken house six feet below.

'Damn,' said he. 'I remember her mentioning a village near the plateau. I hope this wasn't it.'

'You wanted to see the village again.'

'I never saw the village. Don't be absurd, Claidis. I thought they might help us get to the Star.'

We don't talk now at night. He gets either very polite, or surly.

I expect I do, as well.

(Sometimes he forgets and calls me 'Claidis'.)

Although we were in a clearing after dusk tonight, the Star didn't go over. We haven't seen it for a few evenings now. Are we off course?

'Something is tracking us,' he said.

'Excuse me?'

'*Tracking* us. As in hunting us.'

'?!!'

He stopped and checked the rifle. I don't like guns. I always think of the brutal House Guards when I see them. But the Hulta had some. Peshamba did.

'What is it?' I asked.

'For God's sake, Claidi, your eternal amazement about wild-life is ridiculous. Does it matter *what* it is?'

'Yes.'

'Why, for heavens sake?'

'Well it might not be dange –'

'It is. It's something big, powerful and intent. A carnivore. Yes, all right. It's probably a vrabburr – a real vrabburr. Even a pair. They'll sometimes hunt together, a male and female.'

I felt sick.

He said, 'Walk in front.'

'I don't know the way –'

'*Claidi*! I'll strangle you. Neither do I. *Go in front.*'

So I crept rapidly forward, or tried to, cutting vines and things out of the way as quietly as I could.

I hadn't heard anything, suspected anything. He knows all this place and its beasts better than I do, of course.

As we went on, I was aware how much noise *we* made though.

And then we were on the edge of another clearing, a very wide one, with spires of pink flowers and swirls of humming-birds in sunlight.

Venn spoilt it. He said, 'Stay dead still, Claidi, and listen. They – there *are* two – are right behind us. In the clearing there they'll have the chance they want. There's room for them to race and they're fast. What you do is this. You go down into that shadowed area. Stay there and wait. I'll shoot them if I can. If not – when you hear the first shot, run, and keep going. Get as far as you can.'

'What about the ring – rings?'

'Either they don't work or they haven't. I don't know how they work – do you?'

'No – but I can't leave you –'

He turned and glared at me, white-faced. As if he'd happily kill me himself.

'The other village is somewhere here,' he said. 'You've got a chance.'

'I mean – *you* –'

'Oh, me. So what, me.'

'Venn –'

'I ought to feed you to them. Go – *Guljurri ban*!'

163

It was a dreadful curse of some sort. I *felt* what it meant, even though I didn't know. It had nothing, I bet, to do with furballs.

Confusedly I thought, He's going to let them have *him*, if he misses with the gun. He's frightened and trying to save me – this is all wrong – but I'm making it worse.

So I slipped away from him without another word, into the tangled shadow between the trees. I hid, as he'd told me.

I was frightened daft myself, but somehow it didn't seem real, and I thought, Nothing will happen.

Then, the vrabburrs came.

PEARL FLAMINGO VILLAGE

They were very big, that was what I thought first. Then that one vrabburr was larger than the other. A parent and child, perhaps. Daddy or mummy vrabburr teaching baby vrabburr how to hunt.

Sunlight shone on them, but also they were all part of the forest, its bars of shadow and dull highlights on their pelt. So in a way, the forest too seemed to be stalking us, had *become* the vrabburrs in order to attack us properly.

They'd halted, a short distance from Venn. We'd made a tunnel through the foliage, and they could see him clearly, with the loaded gun pointing at them. His arms *looked* steady. He looked immoveable, heroic. (Hopeless?)

One, the bigger one, lowered its awful dog-rabbit-tiger head, and savagely tore up a mouthful of moss. (So they're vegetarian – as *well*!) The other sat there on its fat haunches. It would have looked amusing if it hadn't been what it was.

And then this smaller one – just *launched* itself at Venn.

Yes, it was racing, and the speed – two flying *hops* – grotesque and terrifying – and it was there – it was against him – on him – he was lying under it – and I'd heard the gun fired, the shot had split the sky – but it hadn't done any good –

The other one was coming in now too, racing and hopbounding.

I'd forgotten the rings. As he said, we didn't know if or how they worked – and they hadn't –

This is perhaps the most stupid thing I've ever done. So far. I ran out of cover, which he'd risked his life to send me into. It wasn't bravery – it was terror – and stupidity.

I started screaming and shouting. Every bad word, every mad word – and everything ending *Vrabburr! Vrabburr!*

And I rushed towards them, yelling and shrieking and waving my arms –

The bigger one hesitated. It sat back, and reared up, with its ghastly rabbit front feet – with a rabbit's huge digging claws, I now saw – half raised, as if ready to slap or punch me.

But I'd gone nuts. I know I had this image in my mind, not thought out, just there, just what was going to happen, of running right into it, thumping it in the chest, bashing it on the nose if I could reach high enough –

Oh, it wasn't just for Venn. It was for everything.

I was nearly there – and the one on top of Venn was horribly growling, so I thought the worst, and he was *silent* – and I was yodelling something about man-eating marmalade (I suppose I meant the colour of their pelts –)

When –

The standing-up, ready-to-box, vrabburr abruptly toppled over. It fell, like a striped velvet cushion, and lay on the moss.

Venn had shot it after all, and it had only just realized?

But then the other one, the one sitting *on* Venn, rolled tiredly off him, as if it just couldn't be bothered, and preferred to take a nap.

He couldn't have killed both of them with one (delayed) shot.

I pulled up, coughing, breathless.

Only then did I hear a strange thin buzzing sound, which I now understood had made all the fine hairs rise at the base of my scalp.

What now? Some murderous insect, or swarm, perhaps?

Wildly I looked up and around. Nothing. Even the humming-birds had wisely fled.

Venn sat up. His jacket and shirt were torn, there were scratches on his neck and cheek, bleeding, but they didn't look very deep. He looked quite green, but it may have been the green shadow.

'Venn.'

'Feigned dead,' he said, off-hand, although I could now easily see him shaking. 'It's the best thing, if they get you. Slows them down. They don't like dead meat, much. They can't decide, you see, if you're still worth eating or not.'

'Oh, I see. That's clever. Very cool of you to do it.'

We sounded as if we were at a tea-party. 'Oh, hallo. I've just been pretending I was dead as a vrabburr tried to eat me.' 'Oh, hallo, how fascinating. Well done.'

But I kept rubbing my ears, trying to clear the noise out of them. Venn was starting to do the same. And both vrabburrs lay there, like heaps of orange and black plush.

The people stole across the glade, and I thought they were only shadows, disturbed by tiny returning birds, or the sun and some non-existent breeze moving things.

166

And then there were several of them, men and women, a group. Standing there, just below.

The five at the front took the pipes out of their mouths, and the buzzing whine ceased.

Dark, dusk-coloured people, a skin shade I think is brown, but looks almost blue or green in the forest. Light clothing almost the same colour.

Three ran past me, to bend over the vrabburrs, stroking them, putting some loose things round both their necks.

Another one stood there, bowing gracefully to me and to Venn.

This man then spoke in another language.

But Venn answered, saying something like, 'Howa drah b 'doo'?

Then the graceful man turned to me and said, in my own language (accented but clear) 'The vrabburrs are not harmed.'

'Oh *good* – I'm so *thrilled* – my *main* worry –'

'Shut up, Claidi,' said Venn. But he was grinning. He spoke some more in the other language.

The rest of them were helping load the vrabburrs on a sort of tray, which they then, eight to a side, lifted. They must be strong.

Venn said, 'They think all life is important, Claidi. They heard us, he says, and came to save us, but also to save the vrabburrs.'

'Now what? Are they taking them off to make them into attractive rugs?'

'Of course not. They like them. They'll keep them in the village a few days for the children to see, feed the vrabburrs, clean their teeth and check their general health. Then return them to the jungle.'

I gaped. Well, anyone might have been surprised.

'My mother,' said Venn, 'taught them all that. They're from the village I told you about. So I've got you here, at last.'

Their pipes make a sound that – just knocks vrabburrs, tigapards, jaguars – that sort of thing – out. It doesn't hurt them, though.

I've been told, by Shrin, that the air-harps in the Rise gardens, have a similar purpose – their sound, when they make it, warns the vrabburrs, and other bigger outside animals, off. They just don't like it. I remember now, even the larger monkeys would sometimes go all funny when breezes blew through the harps. I'd never linked the two facts up. (Am I just very slow? Well, I had things on my mind.)

Outside, beyond the veranda, is the village. Small houses thatched with leaves. Carved wooden pillars, painted. The lake is the curved shape of a bean, so Shrin said.

I thought it was blossoming trees growing in it, all that silvery pearl pink. But just before sunset, we walked down, and it's hordes of pearl-pink flamingoes, which have given the village its name – Pearl Flamingo Village.

I've seen flamingoes here and there, but never so many. They say there are two thousand on the lake. Sometimes they suddenly fly up, and there's a sort of soft lightning in the air, as all their wings turn and catch the sun.

Shrin is the wife of Burand.

Burand and Shrin are the only ones who can completely talk the language I speak. (They learnt it from their parents, who were taught by – her, Ustareth, and her machines.)

Everyone is still very respectful about U.

Why? She was –

Anyway, beyond the lake is a cliff. It's not nearly as massive as the Rise, but up there *is the Star*. It's absolutely true.

This evening, as the sun set, out of the jungle along this little cliff-top, *It* rose.

From here it looked more than ever huge and overpowering. It caught the last rays of sun, blistering. You can see it has points sticking out of it all over – like the spines that stick out of the green case of a chestnut. Just like a star.

It *is* a star. Only it isn't.

The Pearl Flamingans come out, most of them, to see it rise. (Its return in the last hours before dawn tends to act as their general wake-up. You see, here it's blinding. Sunrise in reverse, and after it's down, the sun comes up not long after.)

Shrin says they all like the Star, they enjoy it – rather as I recall how the Peshambans liked their Clock, which they worshipped as a god. But the Clock was much more civilized than this Star.

Venn has explained to the village the Star may be going away.

They looked shocked – then resigned.

Burand said they'd always expected this. Ustareth had told them that probably one day it would.

Had she meant to use it herself?

Tonight we had dinner on the verandah with Shrin and Burand and their seven children, and all the household dogs and cats, monkeys, mongooses, lemurs, parrots, lizards and snakes. The noise!

They encourage animals of all types. The animals know it, and take great advantage.

I shared my meal with two cats (*not* the dome-headed

variety) and a tortoise – the oddest creature, with a wrinkled, kind, old face, and in a shell – !

Lemurs swung from pillar to pillar. Tails in everything.

A snake kept coiling round our feet and ankles. They call it Flollu – which means Nosy. It is. (It visited me during the night, stayed a whole hour, taking up most of my bed.)

I have to admit, I love it here.

Venn's being nice.

I am.

These people are *good*. I know I make mistakes about people, (the Sheepers and so on). But this village is just – I'm not sure there's even a word for it. But it's great. And apparently, from all they say, that is because of Ustareth!

Venn looked stunned, the more they went on about it, what she taught them, how lovely she was. He muttered something about they were trying to please him by lying. But then he muttered no, he didn't think it was that.

They have the light, the sort the Rise had. It's from some dam(?) around the far side of the cliff in the lake. They have running hot water.

The knock-out pipes were given them by U, and the collars which they use to keep beasts like vrabburrs happy, while they check them over. (I've seen 'our' vrabburrs, in a big garden place. They're free to wander, just in the collars. Children feed them vegetables, and pat them. The vrabburrs look just a bit puzzled. No doubt thinking, all these juicy kids, why aren't we biting into them?)

There are other things. Foolproof medicines, vast crops that never fail.

They say in return Ustareth left them the job of looking after the jungle-forest. So they do. They like doing it.

They know who Venn is, though he's never before been here. One old man came along after supper, and shook Venn's hand. Said he'd known Venn 'as a puppy' (translated Shrin.) And how were Jotto and the chickens?

This morning I was down watching the vrabburrs, when I saw two girls, both with flowering hair. One had white flower hair, one blue.

I saw another cat too, with markings round the wrong way – white with a ginger under-stripe and tail.

'Shrin, she experimented here, didn't she?'

'Ustar?' (That's what they call her.) 'Yes, she did. The village has many abilities.'

'*Abilities*? Flowers instead of hair –'

'*With* hair,' said Shrin firmly. Then she took me over to a neighbour, and said something laughingly to this woman, who in turn laughed.

And then this woman –

This woman cleared her throat – I'd heard her speak, she sounded quite normal – and then she sang like a bird. I mean birds. I could hear finches and blackbirds, nightingales, larks – and other things, all *going at once*, even those yellow birds that go *clink*.

We've been here two days. Venn's been talking a lot with Burand, and the elders of the village, Old Ladies and Gentlemen.

I wanted everything to drag on anyway. No rush to get to that Star.

Then Venn came in, just before supper, to my little room, where I was talking to Flollu.

'Claidi – can I sit down?'

171

'Try that stool carved like an anteater — *What is it?*'

He looked awful. As if all the good stuff of the village had been drained out of him very fast. And a lot more with it. He looked — looks — empty. And afraid.

'You don't understand the language here. I've kept hearing them say things like *When she was here, and then when she came back.*'

'You mean your mother? Well, she came here a lot, came back a lot, when she was working on the Star —'

'No, not like that. It's their tenses.'

'Sorry, what?'

He scowled. The scowl faded. He was too distressed to be annoyed with my lack of education. 'Past, present, that sort of thing.'

'Mmm?'

'Claidi, they said, she came back. I thought I hadn't understood, myself. I'm rusty with their language. But I had. Came back in the sense of stayed. Not left.'

'— *What?*'

'Is still here.'

We both sat there, staring at each other.

At last he said, 'What I haven't grasped is if they've told her I'm here. I get the impression they haven't. *Can't.* But when I got it straight, I said, Let me see her. And without hesitation they said, Yes, when would you like to?'

The warm evening was cold, for me.

'Is she in the Star?'

'No. It's a building on the flamingo lake.'

'You're going?'

'Wouldn't you?'

Would I?

'I don't know. I never knew Twilight. I'm not even sure

172

she *is* my mother. But if she was, she left me because she had no choice. I don't – I haven't a quarrel with her.'

He put his head in his hands.

Then he got up and walked about such a lot the wooden floor groaned, and Flollu gave a sort of snake sneeze and rippled out.

'They said they'd row me out tonight, after supper,' said Venn. 'So I won't be eating supper.'

'No.' My stomach too was churning.

Ustareth – *here*.

The Ustareth.

'Claidi – will you come with me?'

'Me?'

'For all the worst reasons. I'm afraid to meet her. Afraid of what I'll say and do – what I'll feel. Afraid I won't believe afterwards I saw her at all.'

'Isn't there a chance you and she might – make it up.'

'No,' he said. No rage. Just – an empty space.

HER

A tall villager rowed us over through afterglow and matching flamingoes.

The water here was thickly-smooth as milk.

It was an island, small. Trees already heavy with night, and a house only visible between them. The house had a pointed roof, with indigo tiles, now turning black. No lights, no lit windows.

'Is she there?' Venn asked.

'Yes,' said the villager. I knew that word by now at least.

'She doesn't put on the lights – or light a lamp.'

'No, Venar Yllar.'

Venn was like stone. Stone-voiced. Inside, I thought, churning like I was; worse, of course, much worse.

The boat scraped in on pebbles. Two or three more flamingoes flushed up from the shore and flapped away.

We got out.

'Better wait,' said Venn to the villager.

The villager shook his head. He said something and Venn said shortly, 'Oh, all right.'

'Where's he going?' I asked, as the man rowed off.

'He says he'll sit on the lake in his boat. Come back when we signal. Our meeting is to be *that* private.'

The Star had risen. It was already going away, in over the jungles, towards the Rise. Shadows lengthening and closing like doors.

Venn turned and strode up the shale towards the dark house in the trees.

There *was* no door. That was the first thing. All the windows were one storey up. Then, round the far side, fumbling now in blackness and starlight, there was a stair, which led up to one long window above. He put a foot on this stair, and the hard light came on, blinding us both.

Perhaps I should just have kept quiet, but I thought I ought to suggest this: 'Venn, if we get in, and it's *her* house – suppose the rooms move?'

'Bar jar, lak sush,' he grated.

I'm fairly sure this means, Shut up you *** fool. So I shut up.

The light was in a glass tube by the window, and we went up to the window pane, and looked through into a dark hollow with a floor that gleamed like water. There was no

174

furniture in the room, but a big something crouched there –

'*What's that?*'

'Claidi. It's a box.'

There was no handle on the door. But after he spoke, the door just opened itself.

'It responds to a voice,' he said.

'*Your* voice.'

'It might have done.'

He walked in as I hung back, but then I thought the door might shut him in and me out, so I dived after.

I expected a vrabburr or something behind every object, every curtain or screen, or chest. Nothing was there though, not even a mouse, or a spider in a web.

Lights came on, and went out, as we moved from room to room.

All the rooms had only bits and pieces in them. They were clean, without dust, yet unlived in.

We did pass a bed, or a bed-frame, in a side chamber. And in a bath-place, a long towel trailed over the side of the tub. Venn half went as if to pick it up. Then moved quickly away. Probably she must have used it. *Her* towel.

But she was gone, long gone, as she had been from the Rise. Of course, I'd known it really, and perhaps so had he.

We wandered around. There was a wide room with lots of windows, and in the floor a pale burn. 'I bet she worked in here too. Spilled something,' he said.

We stopped under a kind of tree, which was a lamp-stand with many hanging china globes that didn't light up.

'This is pointless,' he said. I didn't argue. Nor when he added, 'But I'll just try up those steps, there . . .'

The steps wound round, and I kept thinking they'd suddenly lurch apart, like that stair behind her closet. But they didn't.

We came out into an annexe, and there was a big wooden door ahead.

He and I stood looking at the door in the hard light.

'Might as well,' he said. But he didn't go forward. 'Claidi, Burand told me something – about this ring, the topaz. He said it could have done what their pipes did, to the vrabburrs –'

'Why didn't it, then?'

'One has to – think *through* it – I wasn't sure what he meant. But it may be the same with your own ring.'

'My ring wasn't made by Ustareth. It was Zeera's.'

I thought, anyway, my ring hadn't helped me. When I was kidnapped – nothing.

Venn crossed to the door, opened it – it had an ordinary door-handle – and walked into the room beyond.

I couldn't see much into the room. There was a brocade curtain hanging just inside. But a softer light had come on.

I'd just wait, until Venn came out, said *That's that, then.* And we'd leave.

He didn't come out.

Had he found something fascinating after all? Something of *hers*.

After a couple of minutes I called cautiously, 'Venn?'

But he didn't answer.

The sensible thing, of course, was not the thing I did. I ran forward and burst through the curtain.

There was a bench, and he was sitting on it. But I didn't really take that in.

Across the room, under another of the tree-lamps, this one all lighted up, sat a woman in a black chair.

176

She was dark, she had a smoky skin. Very dark hair in a long, thick braid, that fell over one shoulder and then hung to her ankles, ending in a golden ball. An ivory satin dress sewn with pearls. Which seemed familiar . . . No other jewellery, no rings on her fingers.

Ustareth wasn't beautiful, she was magnificent. She was like a dark lion.

I just stood there, in this scene to which I felt I didn't belong.

Then Venn spoke to me. Or to someone.

'She mostly used to wear plainer clothes at home. But I remember this dress. She wore it the day she left. I mean, left for ever. She's wearing it now. That's what threw me, when you found the dress in the closet; in her room off the Little Book Room. How could it have been there, when she'd worn it the day she went away.'

The woman in the chair said nothing. Her night eyes burned, unmoving, unblinking. I had to look somewhere else.

'I thought then,' said Venn quietly, 'she must have changed into other clothes somewhere in the gardens, and Jotto had brought the dress back to the palace, put it away and forgotten it. After all, it's not what you'd expect a woman to wear travelling down through a jungle, is it.'

'No.'

'Why don't you go over and meet her, Claidi. My — mother.'

'Venn —'

'Go on. Shake her hand. I'm sure she won't mind.'

I glanced back at — *her*.

She didn't look as if she minded. I stared, and I took a step forward. And then I somehow saw that what seemed to be slight movement in her was only my own swaying about. I saw she really didn't blink. She didn't even breathe.

She was dead!

No. Not dead. She'd never been alive.

I did go forward then, and walked quickly over to her, all the time still expecting her abruptly to pull me up with some crisp comment, some regal gesture.

But she didn't. When I was inches away, still she didn't. She did look very – totally – real. Her skin, hair. Her eyes did, too, except for not moving. They shone so brightly. There was the faintest scent of perfume. And something chemical – as if she'd been handling things like that.

I could remember Argul saying sometimes Zeera's hands would faintly smell of herbs she'd mixed up, or even chemicals. He didn't mind, even when the herbs were bitter. It was her trade, her gift. He was proud of her.

Shake her hand, Venn had said.

So I leaned forward and picked up her hand. She was a little stiff, the way her arm moved. The lake damp must have got to her.

'She's a doll, isn't she.'

'Yes, Claidis.'

'How vain,' I said, scornful. 'To make a doll just like herself – it *is* just like her, isn't it?'

'Exactly.'

I let go of the doll's hand and looked at Venn.

'But it wasn't, Claidi, all that vain. Just common sense. Since the doll took her place.'

'Yes, I see. You mean here in the village.'

'No, I mean at the Rise. I mean,' he got up, but didn't move forward. 'I mean when she left. She left *this* – in her place.'

'But you'd remember it, wouldn't you?' I said.

178

'I do remember it,' he said. 'I thought it was *her.*'

The roof might have just dropped in on me, on us. Or the whole room after all rushed off in a circle.

I jumped away from the doll of Ustareth in the chair.

'But how could you ever – she's a *doll* –'

'Think about Jotto,' said Venn, stonily.

'Well, yes – but –'

'Jotto was an earlier model. With *this* one she got it perfect. Remember it – she – moved about. She spoke. She blinked her eyes, and *breathed*. And it was all mechanical.'

I shook my head. To clear it mostly, which didn't work.

He said, 'And she never let me near her after that. Never touched me. Most of the time I never even *saw* her – she'd speak only about seven words a month to me – only that wasn't her – it was this *thing*. Claidi – *this* even fooled *Jotto* –'

'Venn if it's true –'

'It's true. Of course it's true. Her final joke on me. Not only did she leave me but she left me – with *this* for my mother. I got the idea from the dress, you see,' he said. 'It's a little clever extra thing she did, to show me how to work it out. The pearl dress went with her – yet an identical *copy* of the dress was still at the Rise. Just like the identical copy of my mother.'

'Venn – Venn, listen – you said it all happened – that she *changed* – when you were two –'

'It did. *You're two*, she said, and off she went, and I had *this*.'

'Venn, she left you when you were *two*.' I was so excited I couldn't stop the words. It wasn't the time to say them, but they had to be said, and probably no time would ever be right. 'Venn, she's *Zeera*. She's Ustareth, and Zeera too. She was your mother, and she was Argul's mother – you and he – you're brothers!'

'What?'

He'd turned towards me, stared at me now as I stared at him. I repeated what I'd said quite slowly.

Then I pieced it together, there in front of him, as we stood in the room on the lake, with that seated doll, whose clockwork had at last run down.

I didn't say everything I'm putting here, but he knows, of course. It was obvious enough.

She hadn't wanted her Tower husband, Narsident, and she hadn't wanted Venn, or she came not to want him. What she wanted was to escape the Rise, and the Law, and be free. So she did everything They'd said she must – grew the jungle, bred the animals. And for herself she made the doll.

I think perhaps she did wait until she thought Venn was all right. He was an extremely bright and clever little kid. She thought, He can cope now. And also she did something to the doll so it would run a lot longer. Seven years.

When it started to run down, it would leave, so Venn wouldn't see. Possibly she thought the doll would just stop somewhere in the forests, and never be found. Or she made it come to Pearl Flamingo Village so that one day, Venn might come across it, and learn what she did – maybe she felt her lie had to end sometime.

She came here, I'm certain, on her real journey away, when Venn was two. At first I couldn't think why she hadn't used the Star, to leave in. But anyway, she did leave. She reached the coast and went back to the land across the sea, the land she'd come from.

And somewhere there, she'd met, that year, the Hulta. She met Argul's father.

Venn's father was the man she didn't want. Argul's father

was the man she chose. All I'd ever heard of Argul's parents had been how well they liked and loved each other. And if Venn was the son she didn't care about, Argul was the son she valued.

Venn knows that. I went all around avoiding it in what I said, but it's a fact. It must be.

She left Venn as soon as she could. Only death took her away from Argul.

Oh Venn –

Oh, Venn.

How I wish I could make it different, or at least lie really well and fool you.

And what do *I* think of her?

I can only say this. I despise Ustareth, fear and distrust her, yet I feel sorry for her. And Zeera – well, I've always loved her. She brought Argul into the world. And Ustareth and Zeera are the same person, but not for me. Not for any of us. Perhaps not even for herself.

It was when he said suddenly, shrugging it all off, (which convinces me it's gone deep as deep inside him) 'Why didn't she use the Star to get away?' that I did think of something else, and say it.

'To start with, she left it here to go on working the Rise – the rooms, the food and everything. But I think she thought you'd leave the Rise one day. I think – I think she left the Star for *you* to use – I mean, the window opened for *you*. So maybe . . .' I chanced it, 'the Star was left for you to follow her.'

'Well, it's too late for that, isn't it.'

'Yes, but –' It was truly difficult for me to say what I said next. I'm not sure why. 'There's Argul,' I said. 'You're half-brothers. Oh Venn, you look so alike.'

'We don't.' Haughty.

'You *do*. Your colouring is different, yes. Not your eyes, though – and so much else – I kept seeing it, and didn't know why –'

Venn had said once that Argul was someone he'd *wished* he'd been like. Now Venn looked down his nose, (like Argul) *I*? I, Prince Venarion Yllar Kaslem-Idoros – resemble a *barbarian*?

There seemed no point in going on with it.

I cast one last look at – *her*, and went out.

By one of the other windows I lingered, until Venn followed me, about an hour later.

We went down through the house.

Lights blazed on, blanked out.

'I hate this kind of light,' he said. 'You see too much, but it never looks real.'

The door, which had shut, opened when he spoke to it, and closed again when we were outside.

A moon was rising, shining on the lake, turning the flamingoes to snow. We could just make out the boat, with the man sitting waiting.

What do the villagers know about all this? Are they in on her trick? I don't somehow think so. To them, she was always mysterious, a scientist, magician. They must have realized the doll isn't her – and yet, in some magical way, it *is*. Maybe for them, that makes sense, and they think it will for Venn. Because they're not bad, not underhand themselves, or cunning. So maybe they don't see it in others.

'Tomorrow,' Venn said, 'we'll get up to the plateau on the little cliff. Get you to the Star.'

'Er, yes. Thanks.'

Should I have said, *then*, 'If it *can* sail, the Star, please come with me. I'd like you to. You're important to me, even if you weren't to *her*. And he will want to know you too –'

But it seemed, then, Venn might have said, 'I'm only important to you, Claid*is*, since I remind you of him. As for Argul and myself, we'd probably kill each other on sight.'

Actually, I brilliantly said, 'Oh look, the moon's coming up.'

And Venn carelessly replied, 'Moonlight. Now there *is* a light.'

THE STAR

Two hours before dawn, we set out.

It – the Star – hadn't yet reappeared above the village. (The time it took did vary, no one knows why, or seems to care.)

Venn said, 'I want to be up there, on the plateau, ready, when it lands.'

I didn't, really. But then, I was afraid of it.

And he was too, and that was why he wanted to confront it. Because it was too late to confront *her*.

The village had been very silent. No one much about.

If it was possible, I'd be robbing them of their Star. No one had said anything about that. Shrin kissed Venn on the cheek. But Burand bowed.

Flollu the snake was in his basket, (yes, he had a basket.) He didn't open an eye when I said good-bye to him.

We'd had about three hours sleep. Well, I had. Maybe Venn didn't sleep at all.

I expected him to be bad-tempered and unpleasant, like

before, but he wasn't. On the rough bits of the climb he was patient and helpful. Gentle. He didn't say much.

I'd thought it would all be a tough climb up the little cliff, but there was a paved path, some steps, also level places where you could just walk normally.

The Pearl Flamingans had been here for days though, apparently clearing away undergrowth to make it easy for us. Generally they didn't ever go up there – it's a sort of sacred spot. Even that morning, the very last part of our climb, Venn did have to cut a way through. The helpful villagers still hadn't gone up beyond a certain point.

We emerged at the top, and the sky was pale, and some birds were calling. The lake spread far below, spoon-silvery. A big wave crinkled there – flamingoes.

But, 'Here it is,' he said.

So I had to look upwards instead. The pre-dawn sky was so pale, too, from the return of the Star.

It was stealing in across the vast clearing where the village lies, and it hung by now quite low. It cast not only light but the shadow of itself, like a ghost. This slipped over the trees, the roofs, over the water . . . Soon it would fall on us.

I'd been looking down again.

I looked up. Was shocked.

Now it was the size of all my hand, when I held my hand up, to see. And now – already it was bigger. It was so bright – the hard light Ustareth had made must fill it up, inside.

All the chestnut-case prickles on it looked sharp as knives – but other things stuck out of it too, bright rods and curved bright sticks and things like little shiny saucers – but they must all be much larger, if you were close.

They were.

The Star was sliding home now into the sky above the plateau. It was growing ever bigger.

And the shadow covered us, very black, all the light left out beyond the shadow's edge.

Only when the shadow shifted did I admit I'd thought we were going to be crushed and that Venn wouldn't move in time –

The Star sank, weightless as a ball of fog. As it met the cliff-top, a slight vibration ran through the rock under our feet. That was all.

It was about – a hundred? – feet from us. Now I saw it was, after all, only about the size of a small house – smaller than the one on the island.

And then, to me the weirdest thing of all, all its light went suddenly out. The whole Star had been switched off, like one of the Rise lamps.

'Let me go first,' said Venn.

'Why don't we walk together?'

'And why can't you act more like a lady?' he asked sadly.

'I've said, because I'm not a lady.'

We strode boldly forward, trembling.

About ten yards away, and with no warning – a round opening happened up in the side of the Star.

Venn and I both stopped dead. And I'm afraid I squeaked.

'Get behind me, Claidi.'

'Why?'

'*Claidi* –'

It was too late anyway. There was a kind of ramp coming out, and something was coiling down it, out of the Star.

'Oh, it's only a snake.'

'Claidi don't be a complete – it *isn't* a snake.'

'But it's just like a –'

Well it was. A bit.

A dull-silver, flexible, legless thing, snake-*like*, (like Flollu.) But now the head was raised, and two dawn-pale eyes regarded us. The head was human, almost.

'Dowth ti nali?' asked the head.

In Pearl Flamingan, that means *Can I help you?*

Venn said something to it.

'What did you say?' I hissed.

'I asked if it was friendly.'

'Suppose it says it isn't?'

'It's a machine. If it says it isn't we can believe it. And the opposite.'

The machine-snake spoke again, now in crystal tones, the language of the Towers; the Rise; the House.

'Good morning, lady and gentleman. I am perfectly friendly, also indestructible. The Princess Ustareth made me. My name is Yinyay. Would you care to visit the also friendly and indestructible ship?'

Yinyay is a doll, a mechanism, obviously. The voice is just more female than male. Faultless. It even pauses as if taking a breath – as Jotto did. (As the Ustareth-doll must have done.)

The face of Yinyay is quite beautiful in its way, and surrounded by a long silky mop of tinsel 'hair'. The hair is part of the mechanism. Sometimes it grows very long, shoots into a corner (the corners are rounded, but never mind) delicately pulls out a tiny beetle or snail, which has accidentally got into the Star (ship), then carefully puts it outside.

It chases moths away from the light the same way.

Venn and I both felt funny about going after Yinyay up the ramp, into Her Star-which-is-a-ship.

'Will you take some tea?' asked Yinyay.

'No,' said Venn.

'Thanks anyway,' I said.

'It's a machine,' said Venn. 'You don't have to be polite to it.'

'What about Jotto?'

'That isn't the same.'

Yinyay waited without comment as we argued, still on the threshold. Then it glided back inside the Star.

We stayed at the top of the ramp, staring in.

I'll describe the Star now, I might as well.

Really it is only about the size of one very large room, that is, the top half is, but there's the lower part, underneath, where machines are stored and the stuff that makes the Star able to move, to rise and 'set'.

The upper room is mostly what Yinyay has said is the Deck (like on an ocean ship). It's all made, walls, floor, ceiling, of this pearly metal – I think it's metal, I haven't asked.

The space is circular, and around three circular 'sides' are padded benches, with sort of metal desk-things against the walls. These are – or have – 'controls'. Yinyay controls them . . . or they control themselves?

You can maybe almost guess I don't understand at all, really.

Ustareth had a room/s here too, to conduct her experiments – I don't know where that was. In the lower half perhaps. Unless it was all done at her house on the lake.

The strangest thing of all is that you can see out of the three round sides above the controls, but only when Yinyay does something to them. It's possible to make them respond to just a voice, Yinyay says. At the moment they don't.

When Yinyay told us this, it seemed to gaze expectantly at Venn. I asked myself if Yinyay somehow knows Venn is *her* son. I didn't feel I could ask.

On the fourth rounded wall are doors which open when you go up to them and say 'Open!' These doors run sideways into the walls. (I'd never seen a door do that.)

Behind is an area with a couch, and something that supplies food, and a bathroom area, and some cupboards with books in them, and also 'instruments' – all of which look like nothing on earth to me. But Venn took hold of one weird thing and exclaimed, all pleased, 'An Astolabe!' However, I've no idea what he meant or what it is, or even if I've spelled it right.

Altogether though, there wasn't that much to see, once we'd forced ourselves to go in.

Venn began to ask about the lower part under the floor (if it is a floor) and could he go down and see the machines in there. But Yinyay said it was sorry, but only *it* could worm through a special hatch. 'The magnets are located there,' announced Yinyay.

I have no notion what that is all about. But it seems the magnets make the ship able to 'fly' and to land.

Venn appeared to grasp this. No one explained. (And if they had, I doubt if I'd have understood, so didn't nag.)

Then though, Venn asked the Huge Question.

'This craft – can its direction be altered? Can you guide it across the sea, for example?'

'Of course,' said Yinyay. 'That is this ship's main purpose, Prince Venarion.'

(So Yinyay did know who he was. A little later, Venn said

to me that Ustareth must have stored such information, and recognition, in the Star, and/or Yinyay.)

Mostly though, we were just astounded. Floored by the frightening simplicity of changing EVERYTHING.

As we were standing there, gawping at each other, Yinyay said it would now go and see to the something-or-other which I can't remember properly. It glided off. Yinyay is also *sensitive*, I mean to human moods.

(I can't go on saying 'It'. Apart from anything else, it's confusing – see what I mean. I'm afraid I refer to Yinyay as 'she'. So, I'll write Yinyay as she.)

Anyway Venn led me over to one of the benches and we sat down.

It was very quiet, but for birdsong outside. Below the ramp, in the open that Yinyay hadn't closed up, the sun had risen. Little sparrows were pecking about only a foot or so from the Star.

Before Venn could speak, I said, 'Could it be lying?' (Yinyay was still it, then.)

'The machine? No.'

'Then – she did mean you to sail – fly – on this Star. She must have done.'

He looked at me. One of the long looks that sometimes he gave me, long, long looks, to make up for all the quick looks, the sidelong glances.

'If she wanted that, it hasn't happened.'

'You don't trust the Star.'

'Oh, I trust the Star completely. And this doll-snake. I trust Yinyay.'

'Then –'

'For you. With you. I'd trust you to be safe. It'll take you – home, Claidi.'

All this time, I hadn't felt that. Probably I hadn't believed it could happen. And even now I didn't. Yet my heart sort of woke up and shook itself, with one great thud.

Home. The Hulta.

Argul. Argul.

I felt hot with joy, and then so cold, as if a fire had gone out inside me. I saw I was afraid of going back. Not the journey – but afraid of going back to my life as it had been. To him.

But why – why –

Why am I so afraid half the time I just *won't* think of it. So I imagine seeing Teil and Dagger, of riding Siree, of laughing at some witty put-down of Blurn's. But Argul – isn't there . . .

I now know he, too, astonishingly, has Tower blood. He's related to *Nemian* – to *Ironel* – another of her grandsons! But it isn't that. Somehow that's easy to ignore.

Even in my head, I can't quite see him. It's like how, sometimes in the blackest of nights, you catch a glimpse of something at the corner of your eye, but when you turn, you can't make it out at all –

'Come with me,' I said to Venn. Boldly, as I'd strode up to the Star – and shaking like then.

'No, Claidi.'

'Of course, you don't want to leave the others? If the Star can be made to do different things, we can land it at the Rise, pick them up too –'

'No, Claidi.'

'*She* went over the sea, Venn.'

'And I shan't. Can't, Claidi. I can't.'

'Why not?'

He shook his head. He looked away. Then he said, 'When

190

I wickedly stole your book and read it, I came to know you. In the only way I ever can come to know anyone, now. By reading about you, you became real for me. And – more than real. I've behaved like a pig all the way here. Do you know why? Of course you do, it's the only reason you put up with me. I don't want to lose you. To be without you.'

'Then –'

'But worse than that fear is the other fear. The fear of a world – of people. All of them real. And no book to read on them to put me right.'

I said, 'But it won't be like that. Not once you –'

He said, with his black eyes, Argul's eyes, on the desk-controls that neither of us really understood, 'I'm the unreal one. Just leave me where I am, where I can get by.'

I said, not meaning to almost, 'Argul –'

'Oh, Argul. Yes. And Argul is also the best reason of all for my staying here.'

'Why?'

'Why do you think, Claidi?'

'But –'

Then he met my eyes. His did what they do in books, they *flamed*. 'You both preferred Argul. Ustareth, *and* Claidi. I can't – I damn well *won't* try to compete with *that*.'

Then he got up.

And I jumped up.

'Don't leave me here – not yet –'

'No, I'm going to talk to it – Yinyay. It's all right.'

And he walked to the doors that open when you say 'Open!' and went through, to where Yinyay was all coiled up round one of the cupboards, her hair in the ceiling, (dusting?), and the door shut.

Everything did change that night. For everyone. In the village. At the Rise. For us. For me.

Yinyay served tea in a while, without anyone saying how thirsty we were. And some cakes and fruit too.

She, Yinyay, sat coiled by the rest area table, and when we reached for anything, a tinsel strand of hair would get longer, and lift the plate or pot, and serve us.

I can't remember what was said, much, at first.

He and she talked a lot about the ship which is a Star. Sometimes Yinyay showed how things worked, and I tried to concentrate. I might need to know.

I was angry with Venn. And that wasn't fair.

And I was sorry.

And.

Presently, in a silence, I asked Yinyay what would happen to the mechanisms at the Rise. No one else had bothered.

'I shall alter the circuits,' said Yinyay. 'Nothing need be upset at all.'

'One thing, please,' said Venn. '*Please* upset one thing.'

Then Yinyay said, 'You want to stop the rooms of the palace moving. Nothing easier, prince. Princess Ustareth left memory for me that it might be required.'

And I said, 'What else did she leave as memory – about Venn?'

Perhaps I shouldn't have. It wasn't my business. Venn wouldn't let it be.

And Venn said, 'Yinyay, I don't want to know. *Nothing* about Ustareth. And I don't want Lady Claidis to know, either. Understood?'

Yinyay's hair fluffed up, then settled.

'I have wiped it away,' was what Yinyay said.

A doll–machine – so calm. I felt my eyes bulging with a cry I didn't make.

Venn only said, 'Yes.'

Yes.

So he'll never know, and I won't. Not from Yinyay or the ship.

But as for the Rise, it seems everything will be as before – except the rooms won't move again. Which seems peculiar, I'd got so used to it.

Then Yinyay made a suggestion. (She does sometimes.)

'Since the ship is now to go elsewhere, there's no need to observe the circling route tonight. Would you prefer that?'

So the Star could stay on the cliff. This one night. And at the Rise, when they saw it didn't come over – they'd know we had found it. Know I would go away. Although maybe they'd never doubt that Venn wouldn't go with me.

He'd said, the villagers would see him back to the Rise. They could travel the jungle-forest in safety. He was glad, he said, they might start to visit the palace again, as they had in his childhood.

Doesn't he see, the villagers too are people – and he isn't nervous of them –

But then, they're not the Hulta. Ustareth left the village too. That must make the difference.

He stayed and dined with me, on the Star. Neither of us ate much, but it was a nice dinner. Even if all the dishes came out of a slot in the wall.

Moths rushed to the cool light in the ship, and Yinyay's hair fluttered them out again.

The village too would miss Star rise tonight.

After we ate, he took me for a walk along the little cliff-top.

'Stretch your legs while you can. Yinyay says it will take ten days at least to get you back.'

The Star won't be fast. Slow, gracious travel. They've decided that will be more comfortable for me.

We didn't discuss what I should do with this ship once I arrive. That is, once I've found the Hulta – who may have gone anywhere, particularly if they're searching for me.

I *tried* to ask Venn what he wanted me to do with the ship.

He wouldn't talk about the ship.

He kept on telling me things about the jungle. What tree that one was, over there. And that huge moth, and that flower, which had opened on the rock, and smelled of caramel.

All day we'd been in the Star. Now he showed me the stars above.

'That one's called the Queen,' said Venn.

It wasn't that large or bright, but unusual; it had a violet glow.

Then he said, 'Ask Yinyay to show you the portraits, from the memory bank.'

'Whose portraits?'

'Anyone's.'

I thought nothing could be further off from mattering.

All the while we were there, walking about, and inside the ship before, I had this ache of tension, knowing any second he'd say, 'And now I'm going down the cliff.' He'd say, 'And now I'm going, Claidi. Good-bye.'

And then, under a tree, the ship-Star gleaming not far off, and the mauve star overhead, he says, 'I'm going now, Claidi. Good-bye, Claidi.'

I took a breath. I turned to him and held out my hand.

He took my hand.

Then he leaned and kissed my cheek. (The way Shrin kissed him in the village.) His hair brushed my skin.

'Farewell,' he formally said. He turned and walked away. At the beginning of the path down the cliff he turned. 'Claidi!'

I couldn't answer.

He called to me across the dark, '*Break the rules*!' And was gone.

How happy I should be. I am. Sort of.

It's been three days now, just time enough, as we sail–fly, to write everything up, sitting in the sunlight through the three cleared walls, as green blurred ground and blurred, pleated emerald sea flicker, miles and miles below.

Yinyay does everything. Is even all right to talk to. When I want to talk.

I did ask to see some portraits, that first night, when I couldn't sleep.

Millions of pictures, like paintings, but not quite – passed before me on a kind of stiff sheet that ran up from the floor. Wonderful looking people in fabulous clothes and jewels.

Who were they all? Families of the Towers.

Eventually I did think, and asked to see Jizania from the House. And so I saw Jizania as a young bride, in her wedding dress of gold, with Wasliwa Star, her husband.

Do I wish they *were* my grandparents?

Well, yes. I'd be crazy not to.

She got more beautiful when she was old, but even so, she had a lot of style as a girl, Jizania Tiger. Her hair was fine and golden, like her dress. Wasliwa was a handsome, impressive black man – nearly seven feet tall! He towered above her in his garments of russet and thunder-blue, his head shaved like polished mahogany. So I wondered if her baldness was a tribute to him, in the House when she was old. (If I *am* her grandchild, she must have been so *old* when she had my mother – it doesn't seem likely.)

I can't claim they are my grandparents. I don't know who I am.

There was no portrait of Twilight.

I've taken off Argul's ring.

I feel awful about that. But the ring itself *worries* me now. Ustareth must have used it to get through the jungles. What powers does it have? And on this Yinyay was hopeless. Didn't know a thing – of course, thanks to Venn, since helpful memories of Ustareth have been 'wiped away'.

I keep the diamond in my bag. It lies next to this book, and the new one Yinyay produced for me yesterday, seeing me writing, and how near I was to the end of all the pages.

Which in a way is the oddest thing of all. That my life has now filled it up. This entire book.

And I thought before, after I escaped the City, everything had been sorted out, and I wouldn't write any more.

Now, I'm glad I have the other book. The new book . . . ready. (I got Yinyay to check it for Tags. Unnecessary, but I was glad she did.) Perhaps tomorrow I'll start on it. Describe the journey back. Try to find something interesting to tell you, my poor friend, who I've dragged all this great distance.

Yinyay just came and said it's dinner. (Rather like a mother, in some way. But I never knew my mother, so how can I be sure?)

I shall squeeze this in. There's no room for more than a few lines.

We'll reach the land I came from. I'll find the Hulta. I'll find Argul. Maybe I'll see him from the air, even, riding his horse, his black hair flying back like wings, and his fierce face, which I can't quite remember, raised to meet this falling star.

And once he sees me, too, once our eyes meet, then – then it will be all right. Despite the Towers and the Law, and despite Ustareth who was Zeera. Despite Venn. Argul is my family, all I need. Once our eyes meet, I'll be home.

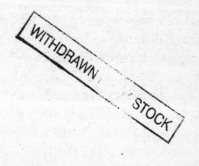